In Love
WITH THE
PL2UG

A Novel By

SHAMEKA JONES

Royalty Publishing House is now accepting manuscripts from aspiring or experienced urban romance authors!

WHAT MAY PLACE YOU ABOVE THE REST:

Heroes who are the ultimate book bae: strong-willed, maybe a little rough around the edges but willing to risk it all for the woman he loves.

Heroines who are the ultimate match: the girl next door type, not perfect - has her faults but is still a decent person. One who is willing to risk it all for the man she loves.

The rest is up to you! Just be creative, think out of the box, keep it sexy and intriguing!

If you'd like to join the Royal family, send us the first 15K words (60 pages) of your completed manuscript to submissions@royaltypublishinghouse.com

SYNOPSIS

Now that the secrets are out, the once tightly knit group of friends is at odds. Four months have passed with no word from Sas, which has Peanut ready to make Em-kay disappear right along with him. Things take a dark turn for the worse when the stash house is robbed, forcing the guys to set their differences aside and come together. Things get even more complicated when Peanut refuses to bury the hatchet so easily and get back to business. An eye for an eye is his motto and when guns are drawn, there's just one question: will they make amends or dead their friendship for good?

With the guys on the brink of an all-out war, Breelyn and Me Me are sticking closer to each other than ever before. With their sights locked and loaded on finding Purple—who is also missing—nothing else matters. Unfortunately, their search for Purple takes a sharp detour the girls never saw coming. Will the BFF threesome take a tragic turn and be forever known as a twosome?

More secrets. More lies. More problems—that's the life you live when you're in love with the plug.

1

EM-KAY

Love? Man, love is a muthafucka. Love will have you doing shit that you never thought you'd do. That shit is so powerful, that it'll cause you to lose your damn mind, temporarily. So powerful, that you will turn on the people you once loved for it. And that was exactly what happened four months ago, when my sister pointed her gun at me.

After catching Purple and Sas in an uncompromising position, I never imagined that my sister would shoot at me. However, that was exactly what she did when I mentioned that she would never see Sas again. I would admit, I had temporarily lost my mind at the sight of them. And I would admit that I wanted to hurt her ass and I was. Still, the fact that she tried to hurt me, hurt me the most. When she let off a shot that grazed my thigh, I realized how powerful love really was. My sister never came at me the way she did. I mean, she literally chased and shot at me. Luckily, she only had four bullets in the clip.

Purple left the house and I hadn't seen her since. At first, I thought that she would stay gone for a few days then come back. Purple had never been on her own before, so I didn't bother looking for her until a week later. However, 17 weeks had passed, and I hadn't heard as much as a peep from her. I wouldn't lie, I missed having my sister around. Half of my life revolved around her, so I was feeling empty as fuck. I was even missing her smart-ass mouth.

As far as that nigga, Sas, I didn't give a fuck what had happened to his ass. That nigga betrayed me in one of the worst ways and I couldn't forgive him for that shit. Mainly, because he knew that the shit was wrong. That was why he didn't open his mouth about it. Purple was supposed to be his fucking sister. He smiled in my face every day knowing that he was smashing my little sister behind my back. Every time I thought about that shit, I got mad all over again. Especially since I had run the cameras in my house back and saw the many videos of them.

Seeing my sister on her knees, serving that nigga up, caused me to throw the fuck up. I was literally sick to my stomach. After that, I went looking for his ass. I paid every bitch he was ever in contact with a visit. All of them said that they hadn't heard from him, except Brittney. From what she told me, she called him on the day all that shit went down. She said that he was in the car with a female. It made me wonder if Sas and Purple were hiding out together. I tried not to think about it much, but it still crossed my mind every now and then. That had to be the reason Purple hadn't come back home, because she hadn't used any of her debit cards.

The one thing I could say about that love shit, was that it was faithful. Purple turned her back on me behind Sas while Breelynn had never left my side. Once Purple stopped shooting at me, she jumped in her Jeep and burned out. I drove back over to the apartment with Breelynn. She cleaned my wound while I told her what happened. She told me that she was aware of Purple's crush but didn't think that they were having sex. That made sense because in every video, Purple looked to be the aggressor. Still, my bro should have been stronger than that. If he would've just told me what was up, I would've checked that shit. But nah, he had to be a hoe ass nigga.

"Here you go, baby," I said, walking up to the bed with a tray of food. "I made you breakfast in bed."

Breelynn sat up and slid back against the headboard. "Thank you, baby."

She was seven months pregnant with my son and I was taking good care of them. Breelynn was pregnant with twins but miscarried one of the boys two months ago. She was placed on bedrest, so Breelynn and the baby had been my focus. I had to keep them both comfortable. Though shit was going on in the streets, I made sure to take care of home first.

A month after everything went down, Breelynn and I eloped. I vowed to always put our family first; therefore, I was going to keep my word. Almost losing Bree caused me to step my game all the way up. I couldn't risk losing her again. Especially not after losing my sister and brother. My family was what I wanted and needed.

"How you feelin'?" I asked, sliding in the bed next to her and placing my hand on her stomach.

"I feel alright," she answered, placing a slice of bacon in my mouth.

Chewing, I replied, "You tryna make me fat?"

She nodded as she pushed a piece of bacon in her mouth.

"Oh, you thought I was gon' be fat by myself? Nah, bruh."

No lie, a nigga had put on a few pounds since Breelynn had been pregnant. Every time she ate, so did I. Hell, half the time, I was the one suggesting that we eat. I was cool with it, though. The little weight I had put on made me look buff.

Just as we finished breakfast, Breelynn's cell started ringing. While she took the call, I went to clean the kitchen. I was just about finished, when Breelynn strolled in. Though I knew that Breelynn was tired of being in the bed, I hated when she was up walking around. All I could think about was losing my son, and I didn't want to lose the other one. Being a father was something that I was looking forward to, especially since I was having a son.

"Me Me and Peanut are on their way over here," Bree advised.

Looking at her with my eyebrows pressed together, Breelynn just shrugged. Since Sas was nowhere to be found, Peanut and I hadn't been rocking with each other too much. I dealt with Reef and he relayed shit to Peanut. Peanut was aware of what went down; therefore, he knew that I was the reason for Sas disappearing. He couldn't prove if I had killed Sas or not, so he just kept his distance. So, you understand why his coming over was a surprise to me.

To be on the safe side, I carried Breelynn back up to the room then hid a few guns around the house. I wasn't taking any chances that he found out something about Sas and was coming to do me in. He had made it clear to me that if he found out that Sas was dead, that I would be joining him. When the doorbell rang, I slid my piece in the small of my back then answered the door. Me Me was standing in front, so I stepped back to let her enter.

"Hey, how you doing, Em-kay?" she spoke.

"I'm good. What's up?"

"Nothing much. Where Bree?"

"She upstairs."

Me Me looked back at Peanut as she strolled past me. Peanut was still outside the door, staring at Sas's car which was still in the driveway. Attentively, I watched him for any slick movements. One wrong move and shit was going to get ugly. Finally, he turned to face me then stepped inside.

"What's good?"

"Nothing," he replied. "Shit is fucked up. Somebody hit the warehouse this morning."

Hearing that shit knocked the breath out of me. We had been in business for a little over five months and shit had been smooth as butter. Who the fuck was bold enough to fuck with our shit?

"How much they get away with?"

"It was like 75 bricks left. They took all but one of 'em. The one they left, they tore it open and sprinkled it on the floor."

"So, they was some disrespectful muthafuckas, huh?" I nodded. "Bet."

I was mad, but not too pissed. The bricks that were taken were all profit. Estelle had already been paid from that load, so we didn't have to worry about coming up short. Besides, I still had a shit load of bricks at the other warehouse. Still, the profit from the bricks that were stolen was going to hurt a nigga's pocket. And with a baby on the way, I couldn't afford to come up short anywhere.

"Whoever it was," Peanut continued, "they were smart. They cut the wires to the alarms without trippin' 'em. If Reef didn't have a delivery this morning, we wouldn't even know."

Most thieving ass niggas weren't too smart, which had me wondering about who could have taken the bricks. I was too good to the 'hood for anybody to try me, so I doubted if any of the 'hood niggas had got down on me. At the same time, I couldn't be so sure. Fuck niggas were everywhere, and it was always one that was bold enough to test the water. Especially since niggas knew that Sas wasn't around. And since he wasn't around, it was time for me to turn up in these streets. I had to remind niggas of who the fuck Em-kay was.

"A'ight. Get up with them youngins. Let them know to have their ears to the street. And to be ready for anything."

"No disrespect to you, my nigga. But them young niggas respect Sas. They ain't never had a face to face with you. No doubt, they'll get down for me, but I ain't orderin' shit until I know what happened to Sas."

"Nigga, you work for me."

"Don't get shit twisted. I worked *with* Sas, I don't do a mutha-fuckin' thang for *you*. So, like I fuckin' said, ain't shit poppin' 'til I know what happened to my nigga. On god."

And here comes the bullshit! I should have known something was up with the face to face visit. The last thing I wanted to do was decorate my living room with blood, but that nigga was pushing it with his loose ass mouth.

"My nigga, I already told you what the fuck happened!"

"I don't believe yo' bitch ass, though!"

Soon as that shit left his lips, I knew that it was about to get real. I didn't give a fuck how cool we used to be, I was prepared to body his bitch ass. His ass was being emotional which was about to get his ass laid out. Obviously, Peanut was thinking the same thing because we pulled out our guns simultaneously and pointed them at each other.

2

BREELYNN

Since Purple had been gone, Me Me and I had grown closer. Mainly, because we were trying to keep the peace between our men. Because of the Sas and Purple situation, Em-kay and Peanut weren't seeing eye to eye. And being that we were both equally close to Purple, we were worried about her. Although Em-kay never mentioned it, I knew that he was worried as well. He was hardly sleeping, and he kept himself busy.

As much as I wanted Em-kay and my son, I would much rather have my best friend back. For as far back as I could remember, Purple and I been friends. So, it was weird not having her around. I would give anything to have my friend back, and that was why Me Me and I searched daily for her then met up to compare notes.

"Bree," Me Me started. "Do you think Sas is dead?"

"Honestly, Me Me, I don't think so. Em-kay said he left the house and his body hasn't been found. Em-kay was with me right after it all went down, so I know he didn't bury him. He still had on the clothes he left in, and the only blood on them was his."

"Do you think Purple is with him?"

"I don't know. But I hope so. Not knowing what's going on with her is killin' me."

"Me, too." Me Me sighed. "I hate how shit is. Everything is fucked up."

That shit made me feel bad because I knew that I had contributed to the situation. If I had stayed hidden instead of going to that pool party, the guys wouldn't have pulled up on us. And if I had just told my friend the truth, she wouldn't have reacted the way she did. Truth was, had I known that Sas and Purple were fucking, I wouldn't have even told Em-kay that Me Me said they were together that day.

"We gotta find her, Me Me. Maybe then we'll find Sas and him and Em-kay can work shit out."

"I don't know about getting in the middle of that shit. Let's just find Purple."

Just as Me Me completed her statement, yelling could be heard coming from downstairs. Immediately, Me Me jumped up and ran out the room. I couldn't move as fast, so it took me a little longer.

By the time I got to the top of the stairs, Peanut and Em-kay had their guns drawn on each other. Me Me was standing in front of Peanut, blocking Em-kay's shot.

"Move, bae," Peanut said, trying to push Me Me away, but she kept stepping in front of him.

"Get yo' ass out the way, Me Me!" Em-kay bellowed.

"Y'all need to stop this shit!" I exclaimed, making my way down the stairs. "Y'all been at it long enough. It's time to find Purple and Sas and settle this shit."

"This nigga killed my nigga and I'm gon' kill his ass," Peanut assured me.

Like Me Me, I stood in front of Em-kay, blocking Peanut's shot. Of course, Em-kay was cursing me out about it, but I wasn't going to move. I knew Peanut, and I knew that he would shoot Em-kay with no problem. He had said it too many times. There was no way that I was letting that shit happen, so I stood my ground.

"Y'all get the fuck out the way!" Peanut growled. "Y'all ain't got shit to do with this shit! Breelynn, move 'fore I shoot yo' ass, too."

"Bitch, you shoot my wife, we all dyin' tuh-day!" Em-kay threatened. "I already told yo' dumb ass that the nigga ran outta here! I don't know where the fuck Sas at. And if you find that nigga, you betta keep that muthafucka away from me!"

"Fuck you, nigga! Yo' bitch ass sister is the reason all this shit happened! That hoe was throwin' that shit at my nigga. And just like you with this bitch, he got weak."

"Who the fuck you callin' a bitch, nigga?" I snapped. "Don't disrespect me 'cause you can't find yo' boy."

"Bae," Me Me interjected. "Let's just go. I got to get to school, anyway."

"You either find Sas or handle that shit by yo'self, my nigga," Peanut said, backing up. "Fuck ass nigga."

Once they were out the door, I turned to look at Em-kay. The way he was grilling me, I knew that he was mad at me.

"Why the fuck would you come down here and get in the middle of this shit?" he questioned. "Huh?"

"Em-kay, you're my husband. I gotta protect you just like you gotta protect me. And I damn sure ain't about to let you die in front of me. I'd rather die with you than become a widow."

"You do that shit again, I'm gon' be a widower."

"Well, that's a risk that I'm willin' to take." I kissed him then he scooped me up. "'Cause, I ain't livin' without you."

"I love you, man."

Em-kay carried me up the stairs and placed me back in the bed. He sat on the bed then began to massage my feet. Ever since Em-kay and I tied the knot, he had been everything he promised he'd be. I honestly had no complaints. Em-kay handled his business in the streets while handling business at home.

"What was that all about?" I questioned.

"That nigga still askin' me about Sas. I don' told that nigga I ain't know where the fuck he was. I swear, the next time he pull a gun on me, I'ma whack his bitch ass. No cap."

"Babe, calm down. It ain't even gotta be all that. Y'all been friends for too long. And Em, you know if it had nothing to do with Purple, you'd be worried too." Em-kay just sat there quietly. "I miss havin' them around, though. I think it's time "

"Time for what?" Em-kay cut me off.

"*Time* for you to put yo' ego to the side and find them. If nothing else, you need to find Purple. It's been four months, and I'm worried."

"Purple knows where home is."

"Does she?" I asked, pulling my feet from him, then sat up. "Does she know that she has a home to come to? You said yourself that you overreacted. She did too, so she may not think she's welcomed. You need to find her, Em-kay. Christmas is at the end of the month, and we all need to be together. I didn't like spending Thanksgiving alone."

"I'll see what I can d "

"No! Find her!"

"Who you think you hollerin' at?" He smiled, sliding up closer. "You must want me to spank that ass."

Giggling, I pulled him in for a kiss. "Seriously, though. Find her."

Em-kay leaned in and kissed me again while sliding his hand between my legs. I happily opened them for him because Em-kay had been tripping with the dick. Ever since I lost the other baby, Em-kay barely had sex with me. He thought because we fucked hard the night before, it caused the baby to come early. That reason wasn't confirmed or ruled out.

Going through the miscarriage was the scariest thing I'd ever gone through. Especially since I had to deliver him. As hurt as I was, I had to accept it. I had aborted two babies and had threatened to abort them; therefore, it was my karma. I just hated that my son's life was sacrificed to teach me a lesson. That hurt would never go away.

"Ss," I sucked my teeth when Em-kay eased into me. "Mmm."

"Shit," he grunted. "Wet ass."

"Give me all that dick, baby," I moaned, wrapping my legs around him. Em-kay was always trying to short stroke me, but I wanted it all.

"Calm down." He chuckled. "Act like you used to the dick."

"I'm not. Give me that shit."

While Em-kay carefully made love to me, I enjoyed every

moment of it. There was no telling when I would get it again, so I didn't mind him taking his time. The longer he took, the more times I would cum. Hopefully, I got enough to last me until the next time Em-kay decided to be gracious.

3

PEANUT

That nigga Em-kay had me fucked all the way up. Sas hadn't been seen since the day all the shit went down at the pool party. Breelynn told Me Me about what happened with Sas and Purple, so I knew that Em-kay had done something to my boy. Not to mention, his car was still parked in the nigga's driveway. There was no way that Sas was alive and got ghost without getting at me. Something was telling me that Em-kay did something with Sas and I wasn't going to believe otherwise. Not unless Sas showed his face.

After dropping Me Me off at school, I drove over to my mama's house. My blood was boiling; therefore, I needed somebody to help me think clearly. Em-kay was my nigga, too. And I didn't want to kill his ass. However, I would if I ever found out that he killed Sas. For now, I was going to let his ass breathe. I didn't want to do shit that I couldn't come back from.

"Hey, my love," my mama spoke as I strolled through the door. "How are you?"

"I'm not feelin' too hot."

"Well, have a seat... Tell me what's going on."

Exhaling hard, I took a seat next to her. There was a blunt in the ashtray. My mama lit it then passed it to me. I took two long drags before speaking.

"I'ono, Ma. It's just...this shit with Sas missin' ain't sittin' right with me. And, Em-kay actin' like a lil' bitch. It took everything in me not to shoot that hoe earlier."

"Koriyan, calm down. You know how you get when you be in yo' own head. Think. Do you really think Em-kay would kill Sas?"

"The nigga was smashin' his lil' sister. Hell yeah, I believe that he would kill his ass." I paused for a minute. "I mean, I don't know. He said he didn't...and I wanna believe him...but I don't know."

My mama didn't respond, so I just sat there puffing. I guess she was giving me time to think because that was exactly what I was doing. I loved Sas like a brother, but I knew that Em-kay loved him more. And although I didn't have a sister, I knew that I would probably kill any nigga that tried to fuck with her. Especially one of my niggas. At the same time, I didn't think I would. I trusted my brothers; they were good dudes, so I could trust either of them to take care of my sister. Em-kay knew Sas. He knew better than anyone that Sas wouldn't fuck Purple over.

"Well," my mama started, "you know he wouldn't kill Purple. She's alive somewhere. If you find her, you'll probably find Sas."

"Me Me been lookin' for her. But it's hard to find them when both their phones off and they ain't usin' their cards. Both of them are smart, so if they don't wanna be found they won't be."

"Ain't Sas from Haiti or something? Maybe he went there."

Honestly, I didn't see Sas getting on a plane flying nowhere, but it was a possibility. I could get somebody to look into it for me. There was only one problem; I didn't know Sas's real name. His first name was some weird shit and I never knew his last name. Em-kay was probably the only one that knew it; however, I wasn't asking him shit. I wasn't sure of how I was going to get that information, but I was going to get it.

"What's the word?" my mama asked, taking the blunt from me.

"On what?"

"Them boys ain't been back around?"

I shook my head. "Not a word."

After the DEA picked me up, they took me downtown. Since they never told me I was under arrest or read me my rights, I knew that they didn't have shit. Most importantly, I knew that I didn't have to answer shit they asked. Like my mama and Sas had taught me, I sat there and listened to the questions they threw at me. Their questions were going to guide me to what they had.

They kept talking about some witness, but I knew it was bullshit. If someone had fingered me to be the trigger man or the one that gave the okay, they were lying like a bitch. I didn't shoot shit, nor did I give the order. Furthermore, if they did have a witness, my ass would have been under arrest. I toyed with their ass for about an hour then dipped. I didn't have time for that shit.

"Well, they either ain't got shit, or they're building their case. Have you been careful?"

"Yeah. Everything been runnin' smooth over there, so we ain't had a reason to wild out...until now. Somebody broke in the warehouse last night and got like 74 keys." My mama's lips formed an 'O' shape. "I know, right? I know I gotta help get that shit back, but I don't even wanna help that nigga, Em. I ain't never done nothing big without Sas. He got a nigga's back like no other, so I don't even feel comfortable out there without him watchin' my back."

"You need to go find him then."

She wasn't telling me shit I didn't know, but I didn't even know where to start. I guess with finding out Sas's real name. I didn't want to put Me Me in the middle of our shit, but still, I needed her to see if Bree knew his name.

"Where is my stink?" my mama spoke, bringing me out my thoughts.

"With Ava. She actin' like she got some sense this week, so I let her have him for a few days."

After sending my mama and Kairo to Disney, after I was questioned, Me Me and I caught a flight out. We spent another week in

Orlando before coming back. Once we were back, I kept Kairo away from Ava for two more weeks. After she begged, pleaded and promised to act right, I let her visit with him at my mama's house weekly. After a month of that then I began to let him go for the weekends. Every once in a while, we still bumped heads, but she hadn't tried to run off with him again.

"Thank God for the little things."

"You ain't lyin'."

I chilled with my mama for a little minute before I hit the streets. I was going back and forth with myself about if I should help Em-kay or not. Though shit was fucked up, I was sure that Sas would want me to help the nigga. At the end of the day, it was half his business. Thinking about Sas caused me to subconsciously drive to his house. I didn't even realize it until I was pulling in the driveway

The first thing I did, was check the mailbox. I was hoping to see something with his name on it. The box was empty, so I strode up to the door. I rang the doorbell then stuck my key in the hole. The key didn't turn which meant that the locks had been changed. That was weird because it worked just a few months ago. I stepped back to look in the yard, to make sure that the house wasn't up for sale. There was no sign, so I rang the bell again then knocked.

No one ever came to the door, but I swore that it sounded like someone was moving around inside. I pulled out my piece and walked around the house. All the blinds were closed, and the windows were locked. When I got to the other side of the house, I stopped at the garage window. It was locked as well, but one of the blades from the blinds was stuck on the lock which made it possible for me to see inside. All Sas's cars were inside with Purple's Jeep parked alongside of them.

Immediately, I went back to the front door. I rang the bell repeatedly while knocking. Still, no one ever came to the door.

"Purple," I called out. "It's Peanut. You in there?"

I stood quietly, waiting for a response. Still, nothing. Something told me that Purple was in that house. Or she had been there and changed the lock. Her car wasn't in the garage the last time I stopped by. Instead of steadily beating on the door, I decided to leave. If Purple was inside, she probably wouldn't open the door from fear that Em-kay had sent me. I didn't want to frighten her, so I took off. But rest assured, I would be back, and I was bringing back up.

4

ME ME

It was the last day of my first semester of school and my head was all over the place. I had studied hard for my final and I wasn't even sure if I passed it. All I could think about, was the altercation between Peanut and Em-kay. It was obvious that they weren't rocking with each other; however, I didn't think it would get to the point where they were about to shoot each other. Then too, I could, because all of them were short tempered.

Regardless, I wasn't going to let Em-kay shoot Peanut. For one, because he was my man and I had his back. Secondly, I knew that they would regret that shit. Peanut was fired up because he believed that Em-kay killed Sas. I, however, didn't believe that Sas was dead. Niggas like him didn't die easily. Besides, if he had died, we would have heard something by now. It had been four months with no word. My grandma used to always say, *"no news was better than bad news."*

Since Peanut wasn't out front when I got out of school, I caught an Uber home. For weeks, Peanut had been trying to convince me to move in with him, but I had been giving him the runaround about it. Mainly, because I felt like I would be abandoning my siblings if I did. Erin was home every day and she half ass watched them. Half the time, they didn't even eat if I didn't cook. My bother Dre was 16 and lil' Larry was 14, so they could do what Erin was doing. But Derriyana was only 11 and Darla was 10; they needed supervision. Kerry's no talking ass definitely needed me around. I couldn't just leave.

"Girl, what you in here cookin'?" Erin inquired, stepping through the front door. "It smells good."

"Some fried chicken, rice and biscuits for them kids. The bus 'bout to pull up any minute and I know they gon' come in here hungry."

"You're such a good mama." She giggled. "You're way better than the one we got. That's for damn sure."

"Somebody got to be responsible around here."

Erin grew quiet. I proceeded to take the chicken out the grease.

"I guess I gotta get responsible, too," she mumbled. "I'm 'bout to have one of my own."

Before I could respond, the kids burst through the front door. All I could do was shake my head at her dumb ass. We already didn't have shit, so why the fuck would she get herself caught up? Where the hell was a baby going to sleep? In the room with us? Hell nah! Peanut's offer was starting to sound better than dealing with that shit.

"Ooh, Me Me," Derriyana sang. "What's that you makin'?"

"Food. Y'all go wash y'all hands."

"I'on want no corn," Precious complained.

"Girl, shut up. I ain't even make corn."

Precious rolled her eyes then followed behind the others.

"Her smart ass makes me sick," Erin stated. "I don't know where Faye got her ass from. Obviously, not the same place she got Kerry's mute ass."

"You betta watcho' mouth. Yo' ass is pregnant. So, what you gon' do, Erin? Who is the daddy? Is he gon' help you take care of this baby?"

"Of course, he is."

I bet you any money that the nigga wasn't going to do shit. Knowing Erin, she probably didn't even know who the daddy was. That hoe rotated through niggas like she was a blunt. One thing was for sure, I wasn't going to help take care of it.

While I fixed the plates, someone knocked on the door. Dre opened it and Peanut strode inside. I tried not to smile but I couldn't help it. He always looked so damn good to me. Like always, he horse-played with my siblings. They loved Peanut because he played too damn much. And because he was always giving them stuff. After I sat their plates down, they left Peanut alone and he came over to speak.

"What's goin' on, sexy?" he whispered in my ear, grabbing a handful of my ass. "How was school?"

"Alright, I guess. I couldn't really focus. I was too busy thinkin' about you and that shit with Em."

"I told you not to be worryin' 'bout that shit. I know how to protect myself. But on some real shit, I need you to take a ride with me."

"I can't right now. I'm about to get dinner started."

"Dinner? What you call what they eatin' now?"

"A snack. It's only eight pieces to a chicken. That one piece is only gonna hold them for so long."

"You cut up a chicken?" he frowned.

"Yeah, it's cheaper to buy a chicken whole than cut up."

I turned and pulled the roast out the fridge. I was supposed to cook it the night before, but I was tired and made chili dogs instead. Therefore, the roast was already seasoned. All I had to do, was add the potatoes and carrots. Peanut stood there watching my every move until I pulled the plastic wrap off the roast.

"Damn, that look good. What's that?"

"A roast."

"What's that white shit in it?"

"Sliced pieces of garlic that I stuffed it with. Now, can you move, so I can work my magic?"

"You stuffin' roasts, cuttin' up chickens and shit, you gon' make a nigga marry yo' ass."

"Talk is cheap, Pumpkin seed."

"Yeah, a'ight."

Normally, Peanut would laugh and chastise me about calling him any nut other than the pea, but he had a serious look on his face. It had me wondering if he was really thinking about marriage. We had only been together for four months, which I thought was too soon to even be considering. And especially since we still hadn't been intimate.

Real talk, I'd been ready to lose my virginity to Peanut. However, every time I made up my mind to do it, something happened. Well, not something, Ava. Every few weeks, she was interrupting our lives with some bullshit. And it always left either me or Peanut pissed off. That was another reason why I wasn't ready to move in or let him pop my cherry. I wasn't completely sure if we were going to work out or not.

Peanut was adamant about me taking a ride with him. So, I put the roast in the oven and told Derriyana I would call her when it was time to come out.

"Where we going?" I asked when Peanut hopped on the expressway.

"Over Sas's house. I think Purple in there. I went by there earlier and I saw her Jeep in the garage. I swear I heard somebody moving around in the house."

"Are you serious?"

"Yeah. If she is in there, she might open the door for you."

Butterflies filled my stomach at the thought of my best friend being found. I wasn't even sure that she was inside, but it made me feel better to think that she was. So badly, I wanted to call Breelynn. However, I decided to wait to see if she was there. Plus, with all the shit going on, it probably wouldn't be a good idea to tell Bree.

Peanut placed the gear in park and I quickly jumped out. I ran to the front door then rang the bell while knocking simultaneously.

"Purple! It's Me Me! Friend, if you in there, please open the door!"

Quietly, I stood there to listen for any movement. I didn't hear anything, so I started ringing the bell again. If she was inside, maybe the bell ringing repeatedly would get on her nerves and she would answer the door.

"Purp! Please! I'm worried about you! I just wanna know that you're OK! That's it!"

Again, I stood there silent, waiting for any type of response. Still, nothing. Tears began to stream down my face when I turned to look back at Peanut's car. I was so disappointed. I was really hoping that Purple was there.

"Please," I cried, knocking softly. My knuckles couldn't take anymore. "Please, friend. At least text me that you're OK."

Just as I turned to walk back to the car, I heard locks being turned. My heart started beating so fast, that I thought I was going to have a panic attack. When the door crept open, all I could do was cry. I was happy to see Purple, at the same time, she looked terrible. I had never seen Purple look the way she was looking.

It had been years since I had seen Purple's real hair. She had a head full of curly hair that she never wore. However, you couldn't tell that she had a nice grade of hair. It was so wild and untamed. The clothes she had on swallowed her ass. She had lost so much weight. But that wasn't even the emotional part. It was the little baby bump that she was rocking. I couldn't believe what I was looking at. My brain couldn't conceive that I was really looking at my friend.

5

PURPLE

For months, I had been hiding myself. The first two months, I stayed in different hotels on the outskirts of the city. Knowing that Em-kay was probably looking for me, I went to the bank to withdraw cash from my savings account. Imagine my surprise when the teller asked me, which account I wanted to withdraw from? I thought she was bullshitting me when she said that I had an account with close to $400,000 in it. A $250,000 life insurance policy check was deposited seven years ago which I had no knowledge of. And there had been weekly deposits of $1,000 over the last two years. I withdrew half the money then purchased a prepaid debit card to put money on.

It was two months ago when discovered that I was pregnant. Since Em-kay killed Sas, I had been depressed. So, when I was spending my days in the hotels sleeping, I thought it was that. However, I started throwing up twice a day for two weeks straight. Once I took a test that confirmed it, I went to Sas's house. Honestly, I was hoping that he was there, but I was left heartbroken. I had spent the last two months held up in his house, sleeping my life away.

"Purple," Me Me cried then hugged me.

Never had I been an emotional person, but I cried too. I had been crying for the past four months. And Me Me's hug just made me cry more. It was something that I'd needed for a while.

"Are you, OK?" she asked, pulling back then hugging me again. "Are you eating?"

"Sometimes," I spoke as I pulled away.

"Sometimes?" Me Me questioned, following behind me. "Purple, you're pregnant. You got to eat. If not for you then for the baby."

"Why? I'm just gon' throw it up, anyway."

Having a baby was the last thing I wanted to do, but I wanted to keep the gift that Sas had given me. No longer could I have him, so a piece of him was better than nothing. I felt honored to be the one to make sure his bloodline lived on. Still, I was scared as shit. I had never held a baby or changed a diaper. I didn't know the first thing to do with a baby. Hell, I wasn't even feeding it properly now.

"Because," Me Me stated then pulled her phone from her back pocket. "Acorn, I need you to go to the store for me. Boy, shut the fuck up and listen."

While Me Me ran down a list of shit to pick up from the store, I went back up the stairs. My ass was feeling light-headed and I needed to lay down. Just as I got comfortable, Me Me strode into the room. She eased over to the bed then sat next to me. She smiled as she placed her hand on my stomach.

"I missed you so much, friend. Like, for real."

Tears formed in my eyes. "I missed you, too."

"Why didn't you call me?"

"I don't have nobody number. Sas threw my damn phone out the window on the freeway."

She chuckled then looked at me seriously. "Have you heard from him?"

Shaking my head, I spoke, "Em-kay said I would never see him again. I don't know what happened. I was upstairs when the shooting started. I think he killed Sas."

"Purple, what happened?"

Exhaling hard, I began to tell her the story from the moment we left the pool party. She was just shaking her head. Truthfully, I knew that I had shown my ass. I thought about the shit every single day. Still, I stood by everything I said.

"So, after we fucked the second time, I still wasn't about to let him leave. I knew once he left that I wasn't gon' see him for a few days. I just held on to him then we ended up falling asleep. Next thing I know, Em-kay was in the house."

"Did you really shoot at Em, Purp?"

"Hell yeah. I was so fuckin' mad, I was tryna kill that bitch. I'm glad my shot was off, though."

"Him and Bree got married," Me Me casually mentioned.

No lie, that shit pissed me off. Em-kay had ended my happiness while he was living his happily ever after. That was so fucking unfair.

"Fuck Em-kay and Bree. Them bitches ruined my life. Tell me about you. What's been going on with you and Peanut?"

She blushed hard as she rolled her eyes. I grew emotional listening to her tell me about her relationship with Peanut. It made me miss Sas even more. Though it got on my nerves, I missed his slick ass mouth. I missed his kisses, the way he touched me while kissing me. I missed his scent and how it lingered on me after we hugged. I missed everything about the rude bastard.

When Peanut came back with the groceries, I didn't even want him to see me. No one had to tell me that I looked a damn mess because I knew that I did. I didn't have the energy to do anything and I couldn't fit anything. I was just wearing Sas's clothes. Which were bigger than they should be because I had lost weight.

There was a light knock on the door then Peanut pushed it open. The way he looked at me further confirmed how horrible I looked. I could tell that he was trying not to look at me crazy, but I could still see it. He strode over to me and handed me a glass.

"Me Me said drink this. How you feelin'?" Peanut questioned, and I shrugged. "You look like shit," he stated then laughed.

I chuckled. "Yo' mama nigga."

"Yo' ass ain't changed. I need some info on Sas. You know his real name?"

"His first name is, T'Segai. He got two middle names, and I can't remember his last name right off."

"Do he got any mail around here with his name on it?"

"Nah, all his stuff comes in a different name. He don't like people in his stuff, so I never looked around here for anything. Why you askin'?"

"'Cause, I'm tryna find him."

Hearing him say that caused my heart to skip a beat. For the longest, I thought that he was dead. Obviously, Peanut knew something that I didn't.

"What do you mean? Are you tellin' me that he's not dead?"

"I don't know, Purp. Em claims that he didn't kill the nigga, so I'm gon' look for him."

Thinking about the possibility of Sas being alive made me jittery inside. It gave me hope. For months, I'd thought that Sas was gone forever. But to know that Em said that he didn't kill him, gave me the motivation I needed to get my shit together. I had been weak long enough.

"There's a safe in the closet," I mentioned, sliding out the bed. "Maybe there's something in there with his name on it."

Peanut didn't say anything, but as I traveled toward the closet, I could see his eyes zeroed in on my stomach. After entering the code, I stood in front of the safe looking at everything. It was filled with cash and two guns sat on top of it. Underneath the money were two folders. I pulled them out then opened the one on top. The first thing I saw was his birth certificate. T'Segai Narum Elie Aujour was Sas's birth name.

After showing Peanut the birth certificate so that he could jot the name down, I put it back in the folder. As we were exiting the closet, Me Me entered the room with a plate of food. Though I didn't have an appetite, it did smell good.

"You need to eat," Me Me stated, sitting the plate on the nightstand. "And you need to go to the doctor and get checked out, so I'm gon' make you an appointment."

"Me Me, you ain't the boss of me."

"I am until you get yo' life. Now eat. It's more in the fridge, so I ain't tryna hear that you eatin' *sometimes*."

Even though I didn't like to take orders, it was exactly what I needed. For months I hadn't been taking care of myself and somebody needed to check me about it. Mainly because I was responsible for feeding more than just myself.

"Whateva," I stated, laying the folders down and picking up the plate. "You better be glad it smells good."

"Baby," Peanut started. "I gotta make some moves. I'll be back."

"Nah, drop me off at home. Yo' moves take hours and I need to finish dinner." Me Me turned back to face me. "Purple, you make sure you eat. I'm coming back tomorrow to check on you, so you better open the door."

After seeing Me Me and Peanut out, I crawled back in the bed and started eating the food that Me Me made. I didn't even realize how famished I was until I found myself scraping the plate. I sat the empty plate on the nightstand and picked up the folders. I knew that Sas didn't want me in his stuff; however, I was going to look for any clues that could help Peanut find Sas. As I thumbed through the papers in the first folder, something immediately caught my eye.

"Certificate of marriage?" I said aloud.

I grew nauseous at the sight of the marriage license. Even more when I saw the bride's name. Sas was married to that bitch Trina. I was aware that they used to mess around back in the day, but married? I couldn't believe that shit. Just as my heartache had begun to subside, it was back to throbbing again. As bad as I wanted Sas to be alive, rest assured, I was going to kill that adulterer if he was.

6

EM-KAY

The warehouse getting hit put a lot on my mental. Peanut was tripping with the hittas which had me carefully thinking about my next move. Knowing that the DEA was somewhere watching from afar, I knew that every move made had to be calculated. Normally, I would seek Sas's opinion on what we should do then use bits and pieces of what he advised. Situations like the one I was currently in caused me to miss my bro a little. Mainly because I had never gone to war without him.

Standing in the center of the warehouse, my eyes roamed from Reef to Monty to Juke. There still was no word on my bricks, which was unacceptable. Too much dope was taken for there not to be any buzz about it yet.

"So, why this warehouse still ain't got no coke in it?" I questioned.

"Em," Reef started. "We been all over the city shakin' niggas down. That shit ain't hit the streets yet."

"I'on give a fuck about it hittin' the streets, I wanna know who got my shit!"

"Bro, calm down. I'm sayin', though, ain't nobody talkin' about it. Like, nobody. But like Peanut said, it had to be somebody smart to know how to cut the alarm without trippin' it. For all we know, it was somebody that ain't from around here."

"So, why you still in the city lookin' for it?"

"E, no disrespect bruh, but we run dope for you. Sas and his crew handled shit like this. Y'all need to work that out, so we can get back to business."

"Nigga, I pay yo' ass to do what the fuck eva I ask. Don't tell me what the fuck I need to do."

My cell ringing cut off the rant I was about to go on. As I reached for my phone, there was a loud bang, and the door to the warehouse flew open.

"DEA, get on the ground down!" one hollered while a million other agents ran inside.

What the fuck! I looked at my boys as I slowly kneeled. They were looking at me all crazy, so I knew that they were just as confused as I was. I had people on the payroll that were supposed to give me heads up on shit like that. I didn't know where all the heat was coming from, but I had to find out quickly.

"Em-kay Hart," one of the agents sang as I looked up at him. "I heard you the big man in town."

"I'm probably one of the tallest," I toyed. "But definitely ain't the biggest."

He chuckled. "Are those jokes free or do you sell them along with your drugs?

"And here I am thinkin' that I was the only one with jokes."

"I already know this yo' little stash house. I'm surprised to see you here."

"I don't know why the fuck for. You just said that this is my shit."

"Oh, so, this is yo' shit? So that means, everything we find in here belongs to you."

"You damn right, so be careful touchin' my shit."

I could hear thousands of footsteps and boxes flying all around me, but I kept my eyes on the agent. I wanted to make sure to remember his pale ass face. If he continued to fuck with me, his ass was going to come up missing. I wasn't going to entertain his bullshit for years.

"Nothing," a masculine voice spoke behind me. "The boxes are full of sex toys and nail polish."

"Check all that shit again!" pale face ordered. "What the fuck is this?" he asked, holding up a box with a dildo inside. "Y'all into some faggot shit?"

Breelynn was preparing to open her sex shop after she had the baby, so she had been using the warehouse to store her product. Also, I had begun to order the supplies for the nail shop that I had planned to open for Purple, before everything went down. Both were opening in a few months, once I got all the permits I needed.

"Nah, I just wanna make sure yo' wife is satisfied."

He snatched me up from the floor then slammed me back down. The punk ass pigs really got off on trying to hurt a nigga. Regular niggas could catch a case on the shit that they did to us freely. I couldn't stand pigs like that. The ones that thought they were big shit because they had a badge. But a badge wasn't going to stop a head-shot and it couldn't bring them back from where a headshot would send them.

"You got a lot of mouth on you and I'm going to shut it, permanently!"

I chuckled. "Damn, I must've hit a soft spot. Don't worry, I got a pussy pump back there with ya name on it."

"Nothing, boss," the other agent said again.

"What you mean nothing? Check again! I know it's here!"

All I could do was smile. It was the first time in days that I was happy about my shit getting taken. That shit saved our lives.

"Where's the dope?" he asked.

"Man, I don't know what the fuck you talkin' 'bout. I'm holdin' supplies for my business. I'm 'bout to turn this bitch into a music studio. Ain't no drugs in here. Whoever told you it was, lied like a bitch." I chuckled.

The agent stormed off then I looked up at my boys. We were all smiling at each other. We knew that it wasn't shit for them to find, so no real charges were going to be brought on us. Not yet, at least. Of course, that caused the wheels in my head to turn. Knowing that they were after me for that dope shit, it was time to make my next move. However, I still had to lay low.

It seemed like we were lying on the ground forever. Finally, I heard the agent that was fucking with me begin to curse. I looked up and he was headed toward the door. Someone was standing in the doorway, but I couldn't clearly see who it was.

"Nothing," the agent spoke.

"So, you got nothing?" a female voice asked.

"It's clean."

"So, once again, your CI didn't come through? See, this is exactly why I told you to wait. You're gonna blow this fuckin' case."

She turned and strutted away, leaving pale faced Agent Asshole standing there looking stupid. Obviously, she outranked him, and I needed to find out who she was. I wasn't going to cheat on my wife, but maybe I'd get one of my boys to somehow convince her to leave us alone.

Once the agents left with their tails tucked between their legs, we went outside. We were all in need of a blunt, so we put four in rotation. Finally checking my phone, I saw that Lieutenant Briscoe had called. Probably to warn me about the bust, but his ass was late as fuck. For that, I was docking their monthly payout.

"As you can see," I spoke, "them boys on our ass. We got a week and a half before the next shipment comes in, so we got a week to figure shit out. I already know that this shit is dead. We definitely can't have the shit at our houses. And we can't move it how we've been movin' it. Everything gotta change."

"My mama got a storage that she don't use," Monty spoke up. "We can put the new shipment in there for the time being."

"Bet. Set that up and have it ready for next week. Reef, you let them Colombians know that we're changin' the location of the drop off. I'll let them know the location on the day of."

"I got you," he replied. "So, what we gon' do about the shit that was stolen?"

Honestly, I didn't know exactly how I wanted to handle it. The last thing I wanted to do, was draw more attention to our crew. There was no way that I was going to crumble my multi-million-dollar empire behind some keys that wouldn't make or break us. Still, I couldn't let that shit slide. If I did, who's to say that they wouldn't come back and make off with more bricks the next time? I wasn't willing to risk a next time, so I had to get it handled soon.

"That will be handled even if I got to do the shit myself. Until then, ain't nothing movin'. Let everybody know that the shipment gon' be late. We gon' starve everybody out and see who still movin' at the end of the week."

"That's gon' fuck with the money on the back end, though," Reef stated. "And we gotta have the money to pay the connect back."

"We been in the big league for six months. You think I ain't save for times like this? I ain't worried about money because as long as I got product, I can make money. I'm more concerned with stayin' out of prison."

Thinking about all the shit I needed to handle had me missing my bro. Reef spoke facts when he stated that Sas's crew took care of the beef in the streets. Though I didn't want to admit it, without Sas and his crew, I was in over my head. I thought that I could be king alone, not even realizing how important Sas was to the empire. He had mind control over the hittas and they weren't moving without his approval. It went against everything I believed in, but I had to find a way to get Peanut back on board. Without the muscle, shit was going to go downhill quickly. If niggas heard that we got hit and they got away with it, it would be open season on us.

After leaving my crew, I drove over to Peanut's barbershop. A nigga wasn't in the mood for no bullshit, but I was willing to do whatever it took to get him back on my team. Pulling up to the barbershop, I saw Peanut and some young niggas chilling out front. When they noticed my car, I noticed all their hands slide into their pockets. Before I hopped out my ride, I made sure that my gun was cocked, and one was in the chamber.

"Let me talk to you for a minute," I stated, rounding my ride then leaning against the hood.

Never removing his hands from his pockets, Peanut started toward me.

"What's up?" he questioned.

Swallowing my pride was something that I had only done for Bree. It was something that I'd never thought I would have to do when it came to the business. I was a boss and kissing ass wasn't part of my role. However, I was in a situation that I did not want to handle alone. I had no idea of who I would be going up against, but I was sure that I would need back up. Hopefully, I could converse with Peanut and convince him to help me without us having to pull our guns on each other again.

7

PEANUT

Word had already got back to me that the DEA had raided the warehouse. So, it wasn't a surprise when Em-kay pulled up on me. I knew sooner or later that the nigga was going to need our help while he was trying to act like he could run shit on his own. Sas had always said that he was the mastermind behind the business, and now it showed. If that nigga didn't need my assistance, he wouldn't have come to me.

"Look, bro," Em-kay began. "I know shit went all the way left the last time we saw each other. You my bro and it never should've went that far."

That was true. I met Sas and Em-kay in junior high school. I stayed on a different side of town but wanted to go to that school because of the basketball team. Though I met Em-kay first, Sas and I clicked when I met him later that day.

Some niggas were trying me after school, and it was Sas that stepped in and said that it had to be a one-on-one fight. When niggas started backing up off me, I knew that he had some type of juice. The type of juice I wanted. So, I knew I had to beat the dog shit out of the nigga, Black, that decided he wanted his turn first. Real talk, them niggas only wanted to fight me because I was light skinned and all the bitches were gushing over me. With one punch, I knocked Black's ass out. After that, none of them niggas wanted none, but Sas made them step up one at a time anyway. One by one, I knocked all their asses out. Ever since that day, Sas and I had been tight as butt cheeks. Even when he stopped going to school with us.

"I admit that it shouldn't have, but I stand by everything I said. Sas is my nigga just like yours. I know he ain't fuck my lil' sister, but that nigga ain't never been disloyal. Never. And him being gone after that shit went down isn't sittin' well with me."

"Nut, straight up, I ain't kill that nigga. I might've shot him, but I didn't dome that nigga. And real talk, I know I overreacted, but you didn't see what I saw. You'll never understand how I felt because you ain't got no sisters."

"But if I did, I wouldn't care if she fucked with Sas. You know that nigga. You know he wouldn't play so close to home then fuck over Purple. True, Sas is a wild ass nigga, but he ain't never been a hoe ass nigga."

Em-kay hung his head then exhaled hard. I didn't say shit. I was giving the nigga time to process what the fuck I had just told him. And if he got his head out his ass and thought about it, he knew that I was spitting nothing but facts to him.

"What you wanna talk to me about, though?" I spoke since he wouldn't.

"The damn DEA ran up in the warehouse today. Luckily, the shit got stole and wasn't there. But something's telling me that they'll be back. They got a CI, so we gotta find out who that is and take care of that. I need your help."

Already knowing what he wanted, I just stood there looking at him. If he thought I was working for him while my boy was still missing, then his ass hadn't heard a word I said. True, us pulling guns on each other went too far. Still, I wasn't going to help with shit until he righted his wrong with Sas.

"Bruh, you know more than anything I wanna off a snitch. However, I told you where I stood. I ain't doing shit until I know for sure that you didn't kill Sas. I wanna trust you, but it ain't easy when my bro been gone for four months."

"Have you looked for him?"

"I did, ain't shit come up under his name."

"Search for Dominican Pratt, Luke Weber, and Adam Colton. Those are aliases that he uses."

"Bet. If I find him, you niggas gon' have to work shit out for me to put in work. Don't get me wrong, Em, I love you like a brother, but my loyalty is to Sas. Straight up."

He nodded as he stood up straight.

"A'ight, then. Be in touch."

Em-kay made his way around the car then hopped inside. Soon as he did, I sent Sas's aliases to our guy, Mouse. Mouse was who we used to track down niggas that thought it was okay to fuck over us then run. If he couldn't find Sas then no one could.

After Em drove off, I went back into the shop. Herb had just finished with Kairo's haircut, so I went to check it out while picking him up out the chair.

"You fresh now?"

Nodding that big ass noggin, Kairo replied, "Yep."

The bell to the shop door chimed. I looked back to see Ava strutting through the door. I wouldn't say that the bitch looked terrible; she actually looked good. It reminded me of when I first met her trifling ass.

"Hey, my stinky man," Ava sang, grabbing Kairo from my arms. "What's up, Peanut?"

"You early."

"I know, but I wanna take him to go take pictures with Santa. Which reminds me, did you get the shoes?"

"Yeah. Follow me."

I started toward the back to my office. Once inside, I traveled behind my desk where Kairo's bag and new shoes were. When I turned around, Ava had sat Kairo on my desk and was all up in my face. Already knowing what she was up to, I took a step back.

"Man, why the fuck you all up on me?"

"'Cause, I miss you. I miss us. I know I bitch a lot, but don't you miss us being a family? Don't you miss us all being under one roof?"

On the real, I did miss some things. I missed being able to come home to my son waiting by the door to greet me. I missed having someone to go home to period. Since they had been gone, the house felt empty as hell. For weeks, I'd been trying to convince Me Me to come stay, but she was giving a nigga the runaround about it.

"It's a lot of shit I miss and a lot of shit I don't."

"Do you miss this?" she asked as she turned around and pressed her ass against my crotch area.

Hell, yeah! Well, not really. I was only missing it because Me Me hadn't let a nigga crumble her cookie yet. Lack of sex had a nigga wanting to run up in Ava real quick. However, I knew that shit would cause more problems than it was worth. Besides, my son was in the room.

Stepping back to put some space between us, I responded, "Not enough."

"Really, Peanut?" She caught an attitude quickly. "You gon' really choose that bitch over yo' family?"

"First of all, watch yo' fuckin' mouth 'fore I have her run up in yo' shit again. Secondly, I didn't choose her over my family, I chose her over you. Kairo is my family, you ain't shit to me."

"Oh, that's how you feel?" she questioned, snatching up the bags. "A'ight, bet."

I already knew that was code for *I'm about to start trippin' again.* And since she was leaving with Kairo for the week, I knew that it was going to be hell getting him back. At that moment, I didn't let it bother me because I had another task on my hand. Although I told Em that I wasn't going to help him until I found Sas, I was going to let the youngsters know to put their ears to the street. Still, wasn't shit shaking until I found Sas.

My phone chimed just as Ava exited my office.

My Me: *I'm @ yo house. When u cmn hm?*

Me: *ill b thr when I gt thr.*

My Me: *u btta gt hr wth n 3 hrs or im gng hm.*

I was supposed to have Kairo for another hour, but since Ava had snatched him up, I had time to turn a few corners before heading home. Already knowing that Me Me would keep her promise and leave if I didn't meet her timeframe, I left the shop and headed over to the east side to put the youngsters up on game.

I ended up shooting the shit with the hittas longer than planned, so I pulled up at the house 30 minutes before Me Me had threatened to leave. Strolling through the door, the smell of food invaded my nostrils. That shit made me smile. It had been I didn't know how long since I'd come home to a meal. Rounding the corner that led to the kitchen, the lit candles on dining room table caught my eyes. Me Me was seated at the table smiling at me. As I strode toward her, a nigga was stepping on rose petals and shit.

"Oh, yeah?"

"Yeah," she replied, standing from her chair.

Me Me had on a red bustier with a matching thong. She had on them thigh high stockings with the little things that attached to the thong. That shit looked sexy as fuck on her fine ass. I wouldn't even lie, a nigga was at the point where I was ready to fuck on her. That oral shit wasn't satisfying a nigga anymore. And seeing her in stuff like that had me fiending to squeeze in between it.

"Damn, baby," I groaned, cuffing that ass as I hugged her. "You look sexy as fuck."

"Do I?" she teased, turning around in a circle.

"Don't be teasin' me, now."

"Who said I was teasin'?" She smirked then led me to my chair.

As hungry as I was, my mind wouldn't stop thinking about her last words to me. Was she going to finally give up the cookies? I didn't want to press her and seem anxious, so I removed the top from my food. Me Me had made my favorite meal: neckbones, yams, greens and corn bread.

After discussing our day over dinner, Me Me led me up the stairs. She ran me a hot bath while undressing me. Once inside, Me Me gave me a glass of D'usse and a blunt then bathed me slowly. She had me feeling like Prince Akeem from *Coming to America*.

"Is the royal penis clean?" I joked.

"Squeaky."

"What I do to deserve all this?"

"What haven't you done? You make sure that me and my siblings are good. Even though you're rude as fuck, you've been a gentleman. Not to mention, you've been very patient with me. I know that you're used to knockin' down different bitches every day of the week, and I appreciate you for waiting. So, the wait is over. Tonight, is the night."

Hearing her say that caused my dick to jump for joy. I had been waiting forever to hear her say those words. Had I known what she was up to, I would have drunk a Red Bull on the way home. I'd been waiting for that ass so long, that I wanted to be in it all night.

8

ME ME

The last few days, I had been contemplating on when I would give Peanut the goods. I had already bought the lingerie weeks ago and was waiting for the perfect moment. That moment arrived when I saw Peanut deny Ava at his shop. Peanut had cameras in his shop, and he didn't know it, but I had access to them. Only because I was there when they were installed. Peanut never changed the password, so I would log in from time to time to make sure no fuck shit was going on.

Honestly, when I logged into the cameras, I wasn't doing it to spy on Peanut. I was just trying to see if business was booming enough where I needed to go to the shop or if I could wait until morning to pick up the money for deposit. Just as I logged in, Ava was strutting through the door. I almost lost my shit when I saw her up on my man, but calmed down when I saw him step back. I was proud of him for that. Still, I could see how he was looking at her body. I knew that I needed to give him some sex because the next time, he may not be as strong to deny her advances.

Once Peanut got out the tub, he took over. He dried off then snatched all the covers off the bed. After laying his towel on the bed, he turned to face me. I only had two eyes; however, it was like I had six. Somehow, I was looking at his big dick, chiseled chest and into his pretty eyes, all at the same time. When Lil' Wayne said, *"Chest marked up like the subway in Harlem,"* he was talking about Peanut. His entire torso was covered in tattoos. Still, you could see every muscle that lined it. *Damn, he was fine as fuck.*

"Get over here," he said, pulling me into his muscular chest. "Kiss me."

I obliged. Peanut's kiss always made my pussy get wet, and that time was no different. He grabbed me by my thighs and picked me up. While our tongues danced around each other, Peanut rubbed his hands all over me. Instantly, I was turned all the way on. Then, he crawled backward onto the bed with me still clinging on.

"You look good, but you gon' have to come up outta all this shit, ma."

Immediately, he began to unfasten the hooks on the bustier. I helped him out to speed up the process. Finally, off, Peanut threw the bustier to the side then flipped me over. I was nervous as fuck. I knew I was because I hadn't spoken one word. Peanut must've known too, because after pulling my thong off, he just stared at me.

"What?" I inquired.

"You scared?"

"A little."

"You ain't got nothin' to be scared about. I'm gon' take my time."

He pushed my legs up and buried his face in my hot pocket. I didn't know if it was because he was going to get the pussy or what, but Peanut was eating my shit better than he ever had. The lashes he was putting on my clit with his tongue had my legs trembling something serious. His tongue was showing my clit no mercy, which made me lose control of my moans.

"Mm. Fuck, Big Daddy," my voice quivered. "Oouu, fuuck!"

"Mm hmm," he hummed, not missing a beat.

"Uhh!" I yelp when I reached my peak. I tried to close my legs, but Peanut snatched them back opened.

"Quit tryna hide that pussy. Bring my dessert back here."

"Shiit," I moaned.

Peanut successfully pulled one more nut out of me before licking his way up my body. One by one, he paid great attention to both breasts, then came face to face with me. By the time he tongued me down again, my pussy was aching to be penetrated. Wrapping my legs around Peanut must've alerted him that I was ready. He began to slowly rub his dick between the folds of my pussy. Then, I felt him attempting to push his dick inside. Already knowing that it would be a bit painful, I held my breath as he eased in further.

"Uhh, shit," I panted, trying to catch my breath.

"It hurt bad?" he asked, sounding all concerned.

"Bad enough."

"You want me to stop?"

"No."

He kissed me passionately while removing my legs from around him. He pinned my legs to the bed by my ankles as he eased out of me. Slowly, he entered me again.

"Shit," I whimpered, wrapping my arms around him. "Oh, Jesus, Peanut."

"Damn," he grunted, still stroking me slowly. "This pussy grippin' me like a leather glove."

"Must be that glove that OJ tried on, 'cause, shit...I'm too little for you."

"Nah, you just right."

It felt like soon as those words left his lips, everything changed. The walls of my pussy opened and were taking all of him. Peanut released my ankles and threw my legs over his forearms.

"Man, I love you," Peanut groaned.

"I love you, too."

He smiled then kissed me again. For the next hour, Peanut made passionate love to me. Never was he in a rush; no, he took his time just like he said he would. My first time was more than I could ever imagine. I damn sure wasn't expecting Peanut to tell me he loved me. Nonetheless, it was perfect.

~

THE NEXT MORNING, we were woken by Peanut's phone ringing. When I heard a male voice on the other end, I got out of bed to get myself together. After taking care of my hygiene, I strode back into the bedroom. Peanut was laying there, hands behind his head with a little smile on his face.

"What yo' ug-lass grinnin' for?" I teased, sliding back in the bed.

"Shid, I got a lot of reasons to smile." He secured his arm around my neck and pulled me into his chest. "You finally stopped playin' with a nigga...and I think I found Sas."

Quickly, I looked up at him. "Really?"

"I got to go check it out, but yeah, I think so."

"Oh my god. Purple is gon' be so happy."

"Don't say nothing to her yet, baby. I wanna make sure before gettin' her hopes up. Don't say shit to her about it."

So badly, I wanted my friend back to normal. I had gotten her to start eating a little, but she still was frail as hell. If she knew for a fact that Sas was alive, I knew that she would get back to her old self. However, Peanut was right. If I gave her hope and he couldn't find Sas, that would just break her down more. I couldn't say anything until I knew for sure, even though everything in me wanted to tell her.

"OK. I won't say nothing. But you better find his ass. My friend needs her baby daddy."

"You already know I ain't gon' stop lookin' for my nigga until I find him. Dead or alive. Don't worry about it, though. I'm handlin' it. How you feel about last night?"

Fluttering butterflies crowded my stomach immediately. Just thinking about it had me ready to do it again. It was everything I imagined and more. Peanut was such a gentleman.

"Last night was amazing." I smiled. "Thank you for takin' it slow. Did you mean it when you said you love me? Or was it the pussy that you was lovin'?"

"Yeah, I meant it. You've known me long enough to know that I say what I mean. I play a lot, but I would never play with you like that. Why you think I keep tryna get you to move in?"

I'd been trying to avoid having that conversation with Peanut because I knew he wouldn't like my answer. However, he kept bringing it up. Eventually, the conversation had to be had, though. He wasn't letting it go, and I hadn't given him a straight answer.

"Nut, I know you want me to move in. And more than anything, I would love to stay in this beautiful house. But I got six younger siblings that depend on me. They don't have nobody else. Erin ain't no help and that bitch pregnant, so she damn sure ain't gon' take care of them right."

"Baby, I know you wanna take care of them and that's fine, but who gon' take care of you? Me, you 18, you shouldn't be worried about the stuff you worried about. I just wanna take care of you like you deserve to be. You already know I'ma still take care of shit over there. And it ain't like you can't go over there every day to make sure the house is in order. They need you, but I need you, too. I wanna go to sleep and wake up to this beautiful face every day."

Peanut was saying all the right shit, but I just couldn't. Not right now. I needed a few years. At least until Derriyana was 14. That way I had time to teach and show her how to do everything I did.

"I just need a lil' more time, baby." I kissed his chin. "Let's just get through the holidays. Christmas is a little over two weeks away, and I got to be home with them for that. Unless you want a house full of Be Be's kids on Christmas?"

"You can have Christmas here if you want to. I ain't trippin' on that."

I smiled as I sat up. "Are you for real?"

Peanut nodded. It would be a gift itself for my siblings to wake up on Christmas morning in something nice instead of the projects. Me too. None of us had ever been in anything nice. They were probably going to go crazy when they saw the place. I couldn't wait.

"Thank you, baby," I said, straddling him. "They gon' be so excited."

"Whateva to make you happy."

"I think some more of this dick will make me happy," I mentioned as I circled my hips.

"Yeah, let me gon' and get that one more time. I'm gon' fly out to Haiti tonight, so I'ma need it."

After our morning sex, we took a shower together then prepared to leave. Before we did, Peanut gave me the keys to his Range Rover and dropped $20,000 cash on me for Christmas shopping. I had never had that type of money, so I was excited yet nervous. Especially riding in his expensive ass car. My plans were to go check on Purple, but I had to stop by home to drop the money off. I wasn't going to risk something happening to it and ruining the first best Christmas my siblings were going to have.

It was still early, so when I pulled up to the 'jects, only a few people were outside. I was honestly hoping that someone saw me hopping out the fly ass ride. Just as I approached the front of my building, I heard someone call my name. When I turned around, some bitch I didn't know was walking in my direction.

"You Me Me?"

I frowned. "Why?"

"Bitch!" someone yelled from behind me then hit me in my jaw as I turned to see who it was.

Of course, it was Ava's bitch ass, so I immediately started swinging back on her ass. The bitch that called my name was hitting me from behind, but that shit wasn't fazing me. I was more concerned with knocking the shit out of Ava's ass.

"I told you I had something for yo' ass," she growled.

"Hoe, I'm 'bout to kill yo' ass!" I shouted back.

Soon as I said that, I was snatched backward to the ground by my hair. My back hit the concrete and hurt like a muhfucka. Ava rushed toward me and I started kicking my feet toward her. I wasn't about to let her get close enough to stomp me out. Then, that bitch who snatched me began to drag me down the sidewalk by my hair. At that moment, I couldn't do shit, but brace myself from letting my ass and back get scraped up.

Out of nowhere, I saw Ava's head snatch back and she was pulled to the ground. Chelle was on her ass. Simultaneously, the bitch that was dragging me, fell to the ground next to me. Quickly, I jumped up from the ground. Erin was on that bitch that was dragging me ass. I grabbed her ass by the hair and drug her ass back up the sidewalk.

"Bitch, you wanna drag somebody!" I thundered then kicked her ass in the face.

Although I was beefing with that bitch now, my main concern was Ava. That hoe thought she was bad enough to pull up on my block and I was going to show her how we did it on the west side.

"Hoe, are you stupid?" I screamed, dropping bows on Ava. "I ain't that bitch you wanna fuck with!"

Next thing I knew, a foot was stomping down on Ava's head. I looked up to see my brother Dre stomping the shit out of Ava.

"Bitch, you don't fuck with my sister!" he yelled.

While Dre stomped her ass out, I looked back at the other bitch. Erin and my brother lil' Larry were handling that hoe. Then, all my other siblings started coming from everywhere, punching and kicking the shit out of both them. I didn't even have to do shit. They were handling up for me. That was why I couldn't abandon them; they had my back just like I had theirs. We all kicked their asses until the sorry ass security rolled up and saved them.

9

PURPLE

I was rolling like a bitch while Me Me told me about them beating the shit out of Ava and some other bitch. Even with me being pregnant, I wished that I was there to smack that hoe a few times. I never could stand that bitch. She thought she was so bad, but she was all talk. That was why she brought back up to jump on Me Me. She got exactly what she deserved, though. She went to do and got done. That shit was too funny.

"Purple Hart," the nurse called out, cutting my giggles short.

Me Me had made an appointment for me to see the obstetrician. She was worried about the baby because I hadn't been eating. However, since Me Me came over that day, I had been trying to take better care of myself. Seeing how she and Peanut looked at me, made me feel so insecure. Something that I hadn't felt since my girls hit puberty before me. I had to gain my weight back. I couldn't get caught looking how I was looking.

The nurse asking me 21 questions got on my damn nerves. She asked me 10 different times in ten different ways, why I hadn't visited the doctor before that day. I told her ass that I didn't know that I was pregnant, and that my stomach just grew last week. She finally left me alone then the sonographer entered. When that big ass head popped up on the screen, I couldn't even believe it. Seeing the baby for the first time made shit really real.

"Aww, Purple," Me Me sang. "Look at that head. Big like Sas's and shit."

I laughed. "I know, right? I can't even believe this."

"Me either." She smiled. "You? Somebody's mama? I can't wait to see this."

Shit, I could. I didn't know what the hell I was going to do with that big head ass baby. The thought of raising a kid by myself frightened me. I just prayed that Peanut was able to find Sas before I gave birth.

"The baby is growing nicely," the sonographer spoke. "You looked to be around nineteen weeks. He's a little bit on the small side "

"He?" I inquired.

"Yes, it's definitely a boy." She smiled, pointing out his penis.

Truthfully, I was hoping for a girl. I wanted to be able to shop and do girly shit with her. However, haircuts and Hooters was fine with me, too. I would just have me a little protector instead of a princess.

After leaving the doctor's office, we picked up some food then rolled to the 'hood. Still, I wasn't ready for anyone to see me, so we just drove around. Man, I missed being out there. Even though it was cold out. Once we got back to Sas's house, Me Me and I searched online for furniture. She said that since I was staying there, I may as well spruce up the place. At first, I was reluctant to do it because I didn't want to spend my money decorating Sas's house. If or when he ever came back, I didn't know what was going to happen. Especially after finding that marriage license. However, his safe was full of cash just waiting to be spent.

"Hello?" Me Me said, answering her phone. "Hey, Bree, what's up? Nothing, over here chillin' with Purple."

I was waving my arms like I was trying to land an airplane. The last thing I wanted was for Bree to know anything about me. And I especially didn't want Em-kay to know where I was. He was probably waiting to shoot me back. Me Me waved me off and continued talking. It took everything in me not to snatch Me Me's ass up.

"Last week. I was plannin' to tell you, but I had to get her together first."

Instantly, I got mad as fuck at Me Me. She, of all people, knew that I didn't want Breelynn and Em-kay to know my business. We had talked about it more than once. She was so adamant about me making up with Bree, that it was about to cause us to fall out. And to think, I was just about to ask her ass to be my son's godmother.

"She's good," Me Me continued. "You should come over Sas's house and check for yourself. It's time for y'all to talk."

"Me Me, get out," I stated.

"Alright, girl." She smiled then hung up the phone. "Bitch, I ain't going nowhere! We are friends. And whether you like it or not, you and Bree are sisters now. It's time to fix everything that's been broken. I'm sick of all this. Y'all beefin', Peanut and Em-kay beefin', I'm just sick of being in between it. I got enough on my plate."

It wasn't fair for Me Me to be in between what was going on, but nobody put her there. Her ass came and found me. I was just fine by myself, not talking to anyone. She wanted to play peacemaker, so she had to deal with whatever bullshit we threw at her.

"Me Me, if I wasn't pregnant, I'd fight the shit outta you."

"And I would fight yo' ass back. Now shut up and go eat something. Feed my godbaby."

"Hoe, you ain't his godmama," I snapped, rolling my eyes as I strolled past her to go get a snack. "You *just* fucked that up."

"Yes, I am." She was right on my heels. "I'm the one worried about his well-being. His mama actin' like a lil' brat. I sure hope Peanut finds Sas, so he can check yo' ass."

Her ass was annoying the fuck out of me. However, I was glad that she was getting on my ass. That was what real friends did. They didn't condone bullshit if it was going to hurt you. Still, I didn't agree with her about making up with Bree because I was still mad.

An hour or so later, the doorbell rang. Since Me Me wanted to play peacemaker, I made her ass answer the door. Though I wasn't trying to see Bree, I was curious as to what she looked like pregnant. When they strode into the living room, my eyes went directly to Me

Me's eyes then Breelynn's. Bree was smiling all hard like shit was sweet. Of course, I kept my blank stare.

"Hey, Purple," Breelynn spoke, waddling in my direction. "I missed you so much."

She was standing in front of me, pregnant as fuck, waiting for a hug. I remained seated gawking at her big ass as if she was crazy. Her ass had to be insane to think that we were cool just because Me Me had invited her over. Honestly, I wanted to beat her down. Bree was glowing, looking all happy and shit, while I had been miserable as fuck. She was lucky that she was carrying my blood in her belly, or shit would have already gone left.

I guess Bree finally realized that I wasn't about to get up and embrace her, so she took a seat in the chair next to the sofa. I looked over at Me Me, and she was smiling like shit was sweet. I wanted to grab both of them by the hair and bang their heads together. It was a lot of shit I wanted to do to them, but my lack of strength and energy was hindering that.

"I'm sorry, Purple," Bree apologized.

"What you sorry for, huh?" I snapped. "For fuckin' my brother? For keepin' it a secret from me? For being happy while I've been miserable as fuck? The fuck is you sorry for, bitch?"

The smile that once graced her face was now gone. She looked sad as hell. Still, that shit wasn't moving me, though. I had been sad for months, so I could give a fuck about her being sad for a few minutes. When she left, she was going home to her man whereas I was going to be all alone. While I cried myself to sleep for the 136th night in a row, she would be sleeping peacefully in her nigga's arms. Fuck her brief sadness!

"For all of it," she spoke slightly above a whisper. "I never wanted to keep that secret from you."

"But you did! I don't respect that shit and I don't trust yo' ass no more. I've had months to sit and think about how many times you lied to me. All the times you had to work. How those were the nights that Em-kay didn't come home. All those nights you stayed over. I'd turned over a few times and noticed that you weren't in my room, but

I assumed you were in the bathroom or something. Now it all makes sense. So, were you genuinely my friend or was I a reason to get close to Em-kay?"

"Purple, don't do that. You know I was your friend. Way before I even started crushin' on him. It had nothing to do with being with Em-kay. I've always been a friend to you."

"No, you haven't!"

The more she talked, the more pissed I grew. Especially because she was spitting bullshit. How could she call herself my friend when she had been lying to me? It didn't matter what the lie was about. A lie was a lie.

"Purp "

"How long you been fuckin' my brother?"

Breelynn hung her head then spoke. "Since the night of your sweet sixteen party."

Hearing her say that caused me to lose all my morals. It caused me to temporarily lose my mind. Quickly, I jumped up from the couch and snatched Bree by her hair.

"Bitch, you been fuckin' my brother for over two years and you wanna say you my friend?!"

"Purple!" Me Me called out, grabbing my wrist. "Stop! Let her go!"

I wasn't even hitting the bitch. I just snatched her head down to the arm rest and held it there. So badly, I wanted to punch her ass, though. I looked down at Bree and she had tears in her eyes. I rolled my eyes as I slowly released my grip. I was really losing my shit.

"Bitch, you wrong as fuck for that!" Me Me yelled.

"Fuck you!" I snapped at her. "And the next time you do some hoe shit like this, I'ma be snatchin' on *yo'* bitch ass!"

"You know I ain't never ran from no muthafuckin' fight, so you already know it's whateva. I ain't even tryna hear that shit right now, though. You need to quit being a bitch. Bree has always been yo' fuckin' friend. And you owe her an apology."

"And what the fuck does she owe me?"

"Bitch, she apologized. She can't help that she liked Em. Hell, we all did at some point. Just like Sas. Em-kay chose her, just like Sas chose you. Should me, Sasha and Chelle be mad at you for that?"

I frowned. "I wouldn't give a fuck."

Me Me chuckled sarcastically. "Bitch, I hate you. I really do. I don't even know why I try to reason with yo' ass. It's always about you. Fuck everybody else, right? I hope yo' mindset changes when you have my godson."

"Oh my god," Bree gasped, eyeing my stomach. "Purp, you're pregnant."

"I know," I snapped, sitting back down.

Bree turned to look at Me Me. "Why you ain't tell me?"

"'Cause it ain't my business to tell. I ain't tell you her business, just like I didn't tell her yours."

"So, she doesn't know about the miscarriage?"

"What miscarriage?" I questioned as Me Me shook her head.

"I was pregnant with twins, but I lost one two months ago."

I didn't know what it was, but something in me clicked. It was like, the mindset Me Me had just hoped on me, had entered my brain. Instantly, I felt bad for putting my hands on Breelynn. I had never hit her before, I was just so mad. Our entire lives, Breelynn and I had been there for each other. Even though I was mad at her, I hated that I wasn't there for her. I guess I hated that I wasn't there for my brother, too, because he had lost a child as well.

"What happened?" I inquired.

"I don't really know. I woke up having light contractions. We got up and Em drove me to the hospital. By the time we got there, the contraction was worse. When they got me upstairs to examine me, he was already coming out. My water broke then he came right out. They were fraternal twins, and he was the smallest. They were able to stop the contractions. I've been on bedrest since then. Em-kay would kill me if he knew that I was up and out the house."

Hearing her story made me think about my little one. I hadn't taken good care of him. Luckily, he was still in there. Without even responding, I got up and went to the kitchen. I grabbed a bottle of the alkaline water that Me Me had purchased, a blueberry muffin and an orange. I was going to overstuff his little ass.

Strolling back into the living room, I saw Me Me gathering her things. Bree was still seated in the chair, so it had me wondering what was going on.

"Y'all 'bout to leave?"

"I got stuff to do," Me Me stated, sliding her purse on her shoulder. "I gotta go check on these kids and make sure ain't nothing went down at home. And Peanut gave me some money for Christmas, so I gotta get started on that. Y'all got a lot to talk about and I don't need to be up in the mix. Please act like adults for a change."

That bitch thought she was slick, inviting Bree over then leaving. As mad as I wanted to be about the setup, I didn't even get mad. Me Me was right. Breelynn and I needed to talk. We had been friends for too long for us not to be able to talk shit out. And being that Me Me was about to leave, we were left with no other choice. I just hoped that things went right instead of left again, because I had no problem knocking Bree's lying ass out.

10

BREELYNN

Seeing Purple after all those months made me feel so much better. I had been worried about her. Especially since Em-kay wasn't concerned with finding her. For a minute, I was thinking that he did do something to her and Sas. However, I knew better. No matter how mad Em-kay got, he could never really hurt Purple. He loved her too much to be capable of that. I loved her too, but I wanted to knock fire out her ass.

Never in a million years would I ever think that Purple would touch me. Certainly not after seeing me pregnant. Then too, Purple was just that crazy. When she got mad, she didn't care who she put hands on. I mean, if she would shoot at her own brother, what made me think that I would be exempt? Still, that shit never crossed my mind while I sat next to her spilling my truth. I had no choice but to let that shit ride because I wasn't in the position to be fighting. And neither was her frail ass.

Purple being pregnant surprised me the most. Me Me hadn't mentioned it, so it was a total shock. And to see how skinny she was, had me a little concerned about her and the baby. I would never wish a miscarriage on my worst enemy and certainly not on my best friend. It was bad enough that she was going through it alone. I couldn't even imagine Em-kay being missing and being able to go on.

Once Me Me left, Purple and I just sat quietly. I didn't even know where to start our conversation, and obviously, she didn't either. Watching her eat caused me to pull a snack out of my purse.

"Why you lie to me about fuckin' my brother?" Purple asked, catching me off guard.

"I just...I didn't want to make Em-kay mad. He wanted to be the one to tell you. I'd asked him for months to tell you. Once I made my mind up to keep the baby, I knew that he wouldn't have a choice but to tell you. Eventually."

"So, Em is the street nigga that you've ben talkin' to? The hoe ass nigga that I've been talkin' shit about?"

"Yes."

The look of anger was all over Purple's face. Also, I could see the disappointment in her eyes. I felt bad, too. For two years, I had been lying to my best friend, when I knew that I could talk to her about it. I should have followed my first mind and told her about it like I wanted to. So, I started from the beginning and told her everything. I told her about both abortions, about my mama being on coke, and about Em-kay supplying her. Being completely transparent with Purple was the only way to start fresh and rebuild her trust for me.

For seconds, Purple just sat and gazed into space after I finished my rundown. It was weird because Purple was never quiet. Ever since I had known her, she had been quick witted. Never was she lost for words.

"I mean," she started, "I get it. But you of all people know that you can be completely honest with me. I ain't never judged you about shit."

"I know. I just didn't want to betray Em-kay. Both of you have my loyalty, that's why I kept y'all secrets. It had nothing to do with being judged or betraying you. I love him and I couldn't betray him. Just like I know you wouldn't betray Sas for me. I didn't know that y'all were sexually active."

"Only because you was keepin' shit from me. You know I've

always told you everything. Sas didn't want me to say nothing, but you were the only person I told when he ate me out. I trusted you enough to know that you wouldn't say nothing. I just wish you had that same trust in me."

"I do. I was just in an impossible situation because I was young when we started. I just wanted to protect him. And you would have done the same to protect Sas."

After that, Purple told me about how things had gone down with Sas. While she talked, she was blushing hard as hell. I could tell that he truly made her happy. Purple had never gushed over a nigga before. Matter of fact, she never liked any guy enough to let him make her happy. For once, she had found happiness. Too bad that it was short lived. Truthfully, I didn't know what happened to Sas, I just hoped that Em-kay was telling the truth about not killing him. Purple and their son were going to need him.

"Sas is married to that bitch, Trina," Purple blurted out, out of nowhere.

"What? What are you talking about?"

"I went through his safe and found the marriage license." She sighed. "How could I not know that he was married? I've known Sas my whole damn life. I don't ever remember him and Trina getting married. I knew that he used to mess with her a long time ago, but married? Now, it got me wondering if that was why Em-kay tripped so hard."

"Em was going to trip regardless. Whether it was Sas or another nigga, he would have gone crazy. That was a crazy day for all of us."

"Now I gotta kill this bitch."

I looked at Purple like her ass was crazy. I mean, I knew that she was crazy, but killing Trina was insane.

"You serious?"

"Hell, yeah. If Sas is dead, I ain't 'bout to let that bitch get what belongs to my baby. Uh-uh. Hell nah."

I was hoping that Purple was bullshitting, but by the way she was looking, I knew that she wasn't. Not matter how crazy her ideas were, I was always riding with my best friend. However, I couldn't do shit to help her. One wrong move could send me into labor. I wasn't risking my child's life for no one. And I would hope that she felt the same way.

"Friend, you know I'm always down for whateva, but can it wait? At least until after we have the babies. I'm already high risk, so I can't be doing too much. But I don't want you out there trying to do it alone."

Purple didn't look like she was trying to hear me. Her ass had always been hard-headed and strong minded. Once she made up her mind to do something, it was going to happen. Usually, I was able to talk her out of doing insane shit, but our bond had been broken. I didn't know if I could connect with her and persuade her to wait.

"OK," she finally spoke, eyeing me. "I'll wait. But once I drop this baby, I'm droppin' that hoe."

I exhaled. "Cool. That'll give us roughly five months to plan the perfect murder."

Purple leaned over and hugged me. "I'm happy to have you back. I missed you...sister."

Hearing her say that caused my heart to melt. Technically, Purple never said that she forgave me, but I knew she had. Purple wasn't the most affectionate person; therefore, her hug spoke volumes. There may still be bumps along the road, but I was glad to finally have my best friend back. Now, all I had to do, was get her and Em-kay to call a truce.

11

PEANUT

"I'm gon' kill that bitch!" Ava yelled through the phone. "And I'ma get my brothers to beat yo' ass!"

All I did was call to talk to my son and I was hit with some bullshit. Ava started going in, talking about Me Me and her siblings jumping on her. I wasn't in the mood for the drama, so I just let her ass talk while I got dressed every once in while I'd say some shit to piss her off even more.

"Why I gotta get my ass beat, 'cause you did?"

"'Cause, you chose that bitch over yo' family! And 'cause you always lettin' that bitch jump on me! Fuckin' that bitch in a bed that I fucked you in for years! Lettin' that hoe drive around in yo' whips! Bitch, you ain't even let me drive the Range Rover!"

"You wanted to drive the Rover?"

"Peanut, quit fuckin' playin' with me! I swear, when I see yo' pink ass, I'ma slap the dog shit out of you!"

"OK. You finished? 'Cause I got some shit I gotta do."

"See, you think it's a game. I'ma show yo' ass."

"A'ight, man," I said before hanging up. I didn't have time to listen to that bullshit, I had more important shit to do.

I landed in Haiti late the night before. The last thing I wanted to do, was pop up on Sas in the middle of the night, so I was waiting for daybreak. Right after getting dressed, I sent Em-kay a text then headed out. He called and agreed to help me find Sas. That nigga had to be desperate. However, I hadn't heard back from him since then. Still, I kept him up to date on what I was doing, in case he decided to show his face.

I had passed several colorful neighborhoods before pulling into a nice neighborhood in Jacmel. Pulling up to the house that I had the address for, it could very well be Sas's. It was a nice two-story, concrete home. I hopped out my rental and headed up the rocky driveway. Halfway to the front door, I heard the locks turn and the door opened. Seeing my bro caused me to stop my strides. That nigga looked completely different. Or was it that his thick ass facial hair was covering what was familiar to me? Either way, I barely recognized him.

"What's goin' down, bruh?" I asked, starting toward him.

He looked around before replying, "What's good? The fuck you doing here?"

"I came to find you." I dapped him up. "To bring you home."

"I am home," he stated then turned and walked back into the house.

I stepped inside, closed the door then followed behind him. Just like his home in Dallas, this one didn't have much furniture either. I didn't know why he bought big ass houses if he wasn't going to furnish them. Shit just didn't make sense to me.

"What you mean, you at home?" I inquired when I entered the kitchen.

"Just what the fuck I said. Nigga, you can't hear?"

"Bro, how you just gon' leave like that? So, fuck all the work we put in and the shit we built?"

"Basically," he retorted before downing a bottle of water.

I could tell that bro was on some good ole bullshit, and I didn't even know what to say. As concerned as I was about the DEA and shit on our asses, I wasn't ready to let the game go. I had been doing it for most of my adult life, so killing was a part of me. A part of me that I wasn't ready to let go of because it was a stress reliver. When Ava pissed me off, all I had to do was kill a nigga to get my mind right.

"You ate breakfast yet?" Sas shook his head. "Bet. Let's go grab something to eat, 'cause we need to talk."

"I'll go eat with you, but it ain't shit you can say to change my mind."

I was sure that it was something that I could say to change his mind, I just hoped that I didn't have to say it. Purple didn't want nobody knowing about her being pregnant, so I would hate to use that to get him back to Dallas. I'd much rather her tell him herself.

Once we pulled up on the restaurant, I texted the location to Emkay. It was December, but it was warm in Haiti, so we sat out on the patio. After ordering, I started up a conversation.

"So, what you been doing out here?"

"Relaxin' and gettin' to know some family."

"Word? That's what's up. What about yo' mama? You in touch with her?"

"Yeah." He exhaled. "She's locked up...for killing my dad. It was self-defense, so I've been working with a lawyer on tryna get her out."

"What happened?"

"He was beatin' her, that's why she applied for a work visa to go to the U.S. When she got deported back, he was there waiting on her. He beat her for leaving and for coming back without me. So, when he went to sleep, she murked his ass."

"Damn," I groaned.

"Yeah, I got real shit to worry about. Not that drug shit."

"I agree, that's some real shit. But it's more than drugs we worryin' 'bout back home. When we left the pool party that day, the DEA pulled me over. Them niggas that we setup on the east side were agents."

His mouth formed an 'O' shape. "Oh, damn. What happened?"

"They didn't arrest me. Obviously. But they've been around. The other day, the DEA raided the warehouse." His eyes grew big. "Yeah, luckily somebody broke into the warehouse a few days before that and stole the bricks that were in there."

The waitress strolled up to the table with our food, so we cut the conversation short. No matter where we were, we didn't discuss business around anyone.

"Did y'all get 'em back?" he quizzed when the waitress walked away.

"Nah. Real talk, I ain't even been workin' with Em. I told that nigga straight up, I wasn't helpin' him do shit until I knew he didn't kill you. Yo' ass ran off and ain't said shit, so I thought the nigga knocked you off."

"Nah, he shot me in the back, though. If I ever see that hoe again, I'ma shoot his ass back."

Okay, so, shit was going to be harder than I thought. Months had passed and niggas were still mad.

"Listen, bro, y'all need to work that shit out. What's done is done. Everything is out in the open, and it's time to move forward. I thought you loved Purple and wanted to be with her?"

"I do love Purple and I did want to be with her. But I ain't 'bout to fight with Em-kay behind her spoiled ass. She talked to damn much, anyway."

That angle wasn't going to work. It had been months since they'd seen each other, so maybe he was over her. Sas wasn't the type of nigga that was ever pressed about a bitch.

"Not even if she needed you?"

"The fuck she need me for?"

"She's not well, my nigga. I went by yo' crib the other day and found her there. She looked bad, bro. She think Em killed you. She ain't been eatin' or takin' care of herself. She skinny as fuck."

Immediately, Sas pulled his gun from his waist then stood up. I looked in the direction that he was pointing his gun and saw Em-kay strolling up. His hands were up, but Sas kept his gun on him. I looked around the patio to see if anyone was looking.

"Nut, I'ma ask you one question before I blast this bitch. Did you set me up?"

I didn't know if I wanted to tell him that I invited Em-kay out or not. The way Sas was looking, he would probably shoot my ass for doing it. I wasn't fucking with Em the long way either, but them niggas needed to talk. For years, they had been tight as ass cheeks, and now they would be connected for life. I just had to make them understand that shit without spilling the beans about Purple. We'd see how long I could manage.

12

SAS

"**B**rother, put the gun down," Peanut spoke calmly. "We in public."

"You know I don't give a fuck 'bout where we at!"

"I come in peace, my nigga," Em-kay stated, approaching the table.

"You can come however the fuck you want to. Yo' ass gon' leave in a body bag."

"Sas," Peanut interjected.

"Shit, you know I keep my shit on me, so it ain't nothing," Em retorted.

"Go 'head," I said, taking one step forward. "Try and pull that shit. I dare yo' ass."

We stared each other down for a hot minute. The entire time, my finger was pressed against the trigger. I was waiting for that nigga to reach for that bullshit ass .38 he always carried, so I could have a reason to knock his ass off. That nigga shot me, and I wanted my damn shot back.

After Em-kay shot me in my shoulder, I made my way a few houses down and stole a car. I drove to the only place I knew I wouldn't be found and where I could get some help Helaina's.

Helaina was a nurse and she just so happened to be Homer's daughter. She was a nurse at the county jail. That was where I first met her.

Of course, I was knocking her down while I did a little bid there. That was when I found out that she was Homer's daughter. She would feed me information on who was coming through snitching, stuff like that. That was how I got the upper hand on jobs. I could easily find out who the snitch was, murk his ass and get my paper. She was also the one that told me about Estelle's place in Colombia. She fixed me up and the next day I flew to Haiti.

"Sas," Peanut called out, and I turned my gun on him.

"Hoe, you ain't answer my question."

"Yeah, I told him I was comin' to find you. Hell, with all yo' aliases, he the only reason I was able to find yo' ass."

"'Cause, I didn't want to be found, nigga. And y'all wasted y'all's time comin' way over here, 'cause I ain't going back to help with shit. Peanut, get yo' ass up and take me home. Now!"

I strolled off and headed to the car. If he didn't hurry his ass up, I was going to catch a cab. I wasn't in a friendly mood. Honestly, a nigga was mad about the pop-up shit. I didn't mind talking to Peanut, but I didn't have shit to say to Em-kay. He wasn't trying to hear a word I was saying four months ago; therefore, I didn't want to hear nothing he had to say. He only came because he needed my help and he was going to leave needing it. I wasn't helping that hoe with shit.

"I oughta knock yo' shit against that window," I started as we drove up the street. "The fuck was you thinkin', bringin' that nigga to me? Huh?"

"My nigga, I know you mad, but chill with the threats and shit. And I didn't bring him to you, he brought his damn self. I just told him I was coming and where I'd be at. Y'all need to talk like men, so we can handle this business like men. Fuck this petty ass shit."

"Man, I told you I'on want no parts of that shit."

"Whether you want to or not, nigga you in it. You helped start this shit. And you brought me in. When the DEA picked me up, they dropped yo' name, nigga. They say that they know that me and you organized the hit. They can't prove it, but they know something. We got business to handle. Straight up."

Peanut was right. I did bring him into the business. And it wasn't right for me to leave him and the others out there to swim on their own. Still, I didn't want to. Helping them meant helping Em-kay as well, and I didn't want to help that hoe. He always complained about how I did shit, anyway. Let that muthafucka do the shit on his own, since he thought he was big shit.

When we pulled back up to my crib and Em was behind us, I pulled my gun back out. There was no way that I was going to let him catch me slipping again. I was going to catch his ass. I didn't trust that nigga to not try me. Once inside, we all stood in the foyer looking at each other.

"Look," Em started, "I ain't mean to shoot you, my nigga. I just... when I saw y'all like that, I lost my shit. Nigga, you was fuckin' my lil' sister."

"So," I replied.

"See," Em stated, waving his thumb toward me. "I don't even know why I bother. This nigga fuckin' my lil' sister and don't see nothing wrong with it. I see what kinda shit you on."

"I told you, it wasn't even like that. It ain't like I been waitin' to fuck her or something. The night you left for Colombia, the night of her birthday, she confessed her crush on me. She was tellin' me how she was in love with me and shit. That she wanted me to be her first. I tried to push her away, but she wouldn't let it go. Shid...and a nigga got caught up."

"So, why you just ain't tell me that?"

I smirked. "Because of this shit here. Because of everything that already happened. Tell me that yo' reaction would've been different if I had told you. Straight up."

He stood there silent. Just like I thought. No matter how I would have gone to him, shit would have turned ugly. I knew it, that was why I couldn't bring myself to tell him. I already knew that he was going to try to kill me behind her ass. I had said it from day one.

"I can't say my reaction would've been different, but I would've respected yo' honesty. Instead you wanna lie to my face and sneak around and shit."

"Like you were with Breelynn? You did that for what? Two years? Nigga don't talk to me about sneakin' around, when you been fuckin' that bitch since she was illegal. At least Purple is eighteen. She grown now. She can do what the fuck she wants to, just like I can."

"You care so much about my sister, where she at, huh? Why she ain't here with you? You told me that you loved her, but you ran off and left her. My sister shot at me behind yo' ass, and you ain't even stick around to see if she was good. What type of love is that?"

I gripped my gun. "I couldn't do shit with you shootin' at me."

"What you want me to say, Sas? I'm sorry? I'm sorry for tryna kill you, a'ight? But you ain't die. I just wanna get past this shit, so I can get back to business."

"So, you only here 'cause you need me?"

"Nigga, I don't need you. I only came to prove to Peanut that I didn't kill yo' ass. He said he would help find out who took my shit after he found out what happened to you."

"Well, y'all got y'all answer. Now get the fuck out my shit."

"Bet. Come on, Nut."

"Nah," Peanut said, standing in place. "I ain't leavin' without Sas. I promised Me Me that I would bring you back, so I ain't leavin' without you, bro."

"And why the fuck would you be promising Me Me some shit about me for?"

"'Cause," he hesitantly stated. "Like I was tellin' you at the restaurant, Purple ain't well."

"What you mean, she ain't well?" Em-kay questioned. "Where you see my sister?"

Peanut just started at me. It was something that the nigga wasn't saying, and it was about to piss me off. I didn't understand why Peanut was suddenly pressing so hard about me being with Purple. He was the one that told me that she had me slipping. And she did. If it wasn't for her persistent, persuasive ass, I would have never got caught on top of her that day. She had me going against my first mind which was the main reason I needed to stay away from her. She fucked with my head too much.

"Nigga if you don't say something, I'm gon' shoot *yo'* dumb ass," I threatened Peanut.

"Man, I ain't even 'pose to be sayin' shit." He sighed. "Purple pregnant."

I swore my head started swimming and my damn ears started ringing when he said that shit.

"What?" Em-kay bellowed. "You got my sister pregnant, nigga?"

Wham! He ended his statement, punching me dead in my jaw.

Pow! I responded by shooting his ass. *Muthafucka!*

13

EM-KAY

"Ahh!" I cried out as the hot bullet pierced through my skin.

"Sas!" Peanut yelled, snatching the gun from him. "What the fuck?"

"Fuck that nigga," he stated then turned to walk away.

Sas had shot me in the shoulder and I was bleeding like a bitch. I used my hand to cover the wound then Peanut pulled his shirt off and pressed it against the wound.

"Y'all niggas trippin'," Peanut complained. "I ain't come all the way over here for this bullshit. Y'all on some whole other shit."

"Peanut, for real, my sister pregnant?"

"Man, I didn't want you to find out like this. She ain't even want me to tell nobody. But, yeah, she's pregnant. And she look sick. She skinny as fuck. Me Me was supposed to take her to the doctor yesterday to get her checked out."

Listening to Peanut talk about Purple, made me feel bad as hell. I had always been my sister's provider and caretaker. My ego had gotten the best of me, causing me not to give a fuck about her whereabouts. Honestly, I thought that she was hiding out with Sas. But to hear that she was pregnant and sickly, had me worried about her. Worried about what she had gone through the last four months without me. She had never been on her own, so she was probably clueless out there.

While Peanut helped me up from the floor, there was a knock at Sas's door. Not knowing what that nigga was up to had me on edge. He had shot me in my right shoulder, so my trigger finger was out of commission. If he was planning to knock me off, he was able to do it without a fight. Sas strolled into the living room where we had gone, with an older lady walking behind him.

"This my aunt Lovely, she'll fix you up," Sas stated before walking off.

She motioned for Peanut to help me up and follow her. Peanut helped me onto the kitchen's island, and after that, I was out cold.

When I finally came to, I was in a dark room. The only light was coming from the outside of the house. Soon as I tried to move, pain shot through my shoulder.

"Ahh, shit," I grunted.

"Yeah, that's exactly how I felt, nigga."

I couldn't see Sas, but I knew that he was somewhere in the room.

"I said I was sorry, bruh," I groaned. "You ain't have to shoot me."

"Keep yo' muhfuckin' hands to yo' self."

"*Nigga,* you got my lil' sister pregnant. And she been by her fuckin' self for four months."

"Who fault is that, that she's been by herself? Where the fuck you been? Why you ain't know?"

I sat there silently, looking at the light through the window. I didn't want to tell him that I didn't know where she was and that I hadn't even bothered to look. As protective as I was over her, that shit was crazy to say aloud. I couldn't believe it myself. I guess with everything that was going on with Breelynn and the babies, I just shut her out my mind. She didn't want to be found; therefore, I didn't go searching for Purple. I felt like, if she wanted to come home, she would do just that.

"Em?"

"It's yo' fault that she been by herself, nigga. She thought I killed you and she tried to kill me. When she left, I thought she was with you. That's why I ain't know shit."

"On some real shit, my nigga, you don't never take accountability for *shit!* You tryna put all the blame on me. Yeah, it was wrong for me to fuck Purp and not tell you. I own that shit. But she came to *me*, telling me that she was in love with *me* and wanted *me* to take her virginity. And you tripped all the way the fuck out. I'm not the only one responsible for what the fuck happened. She wanted that shit. I just gave her what she wanted."

"Nigga, you nutted in my sister, bitch!"

"So! I'on give a fuck!"

A few tears slipped down my face as I thought about that shit. The images of them fucking on my sofa began to play in my head. I hated it, too. That shit was forever sketched in my memory.

"I ain't even fuck her ass that many times," Sas continued. "I don't know how the fuck she got pregnant. Man, that day was our second time gettin' together."

"Man," my voice cracked. "That's my lil' sister."

The light flipped on, blinding the fuck out of me.

"You cryin', my nigga?"

I blinked a few times until my eyes adjusted to the light. Then, I turned my head in the direction I heard Sas's voice coming from. He was seated in a chair by the door.

"You got this bright ass light on, fuckin' with my eyes."

"Nah, nigga, yo' ass cryin'."

"That's my boo, man. That's my heart. I just can't believe she pregnant."

"Me, either, shid. Fuuck," he grunted. "I don't even know what to say."

"You told me that you loved her."

"I do. I ain't even realize it until like a week before everything went down. She crazy as fuck, though. I feel sorry for this baby. Being raised by us." He chuckled nervously. "I sure hope we don't fuck this kid up, man."

Sas and Purple were definitely going to fuck that kid up. Luckily, my son would arrive first, and I could teach them a thing or two about parenting.

"So, you comin' back to Dallas?"

He flicked his lighter then lit up a blunt. While he puffed on it, he just looked at me. I knew damn well that he wasn't thinking about bringing Purple to Haiti with him. No matter what went on or how mad I was, my sister wasn't leaving the state, let alone the country. Finally, Sas stood up from the chair and strode up next to the bed.

"I guess I ain't got a choice," he said, passing me the blunt. "A nigga 'bout to be a daddy and shit."

While we passed the blunt back and forth, we made small talk. Once we were high, I updated him on me and Bree, and about the baby we lost. Seeing my son being born deceased, caused me to think about the babies we had aborted. I was forced to come face to face with reality. Guilt was all over me. That was probably why I was so protective over Bree and the baby that she was still carrying. Losing a child, changed a lot of things in me.

Some time after our smoke session, I had dozed off. I was woken by my cell ringing on the nightstand.

"Hello?"

"Hey, baby," Bree spoke. "How's everything going?"

"Well, I caught up with Sas."

"Really? Did y'all talk?"

"Yeah. After his bitch ass shot me."

"Shot you! What the fuck?"

"Bree, calm down. Ain't no need for you to get worked up. I'm good. How you doing?"

"I'm OK. Lonely, laying in this bed alone. When are you coming back?"

"I'll be back tomorrow. Check it. When I get back, you know we got a lot of business to handle. I'm probably gon' be in the streets heavy and I don't want you trippin' about it. It's only gon' be for a lil' minute. Once I get everything straight, we back where we left off. Can you get with it?"

"Yeah, I'm with it. Handle yo' business, bae."

"I love you, Breelynn Hart."

"I love you too, Em-kay Hart."

I talked to Breelynn until she fell asleep on me. Just as I hung up on her, Sas came in the room to get me. We went down to the kitchen where Peanut was seated at the table. A seafood feast was sat out with a few bottles of Ace of Spades. A nigga was hungry was fuck, so I sat right down and dug in. I was still in a little pain, but after a few glasses of champagne, the pain began to subside.

"So, I been thinkin'," Sas spoke. "We know for a fact that us three ain't talked to the DEA or take the drugs. Has anybody in the crew been movin' funny?"

"Nah," I replied. "Shit been straight. Besides, Reef, Monty and Juke was at the warehouse when the DEA ran in. The drugs had been gone, so if they was snitchin', they wouldn't have sent them there."

"True."

"I think one of them old heads don' got caught up," Peanut mentioned. "They probably got hemmed up and turned snitch."

"Probably that bitch ass, Garrett." Sas nodded. "It's something about that nigga that I don't trust."

"Before we do anything, we gotta be absolutely positive about who we hittin'. We got one chance to get at 'em. And being that it's a CI, we gotta do it right. It can't be sloppy. And it can't point back to us in any way."

"What about the dope?" Peanut inquired.

"I want you to get with Monty and them young niggas. I'm gon' starve them old heads out to see if one of them holdin' on to it. While they waitin', I got some young niggas that's been waiting to be put into the drug shit, so I'm gon' have them run a few spots. Just something to keep the cash flow going and to see what they can do. I'm tryna breed the next generation for myself. It's only a matter of time before them old heads back out or die off anyway. We gotta setup our backup plan."

"I got some youngins in the east that you can push through, too. I been told you that I've been training and preparin' them youngins for it all."

"Well, soon as we touchdown, we gon' hit the streets runnin'."

We raised our glasses then downed our drinks. No lie, it felt so good to have my brothers back. Although I wanted to beat the shit out of Peanut and shoot Sas's ass again, I was glad that we came together and settled shit. I knew that I considered myself the kingpin; however, I couldn't do the shit without my brothers. Without them, there was no me. That was like trying to ride a bike with no chain. The crew was the link that connected and kept the business rolling. I now understood that, and it humbled me.

14

PURPLE

I stood to the side in the living room, watching the delivery guys remove Sas's trap house furniture and bring in the leather sectional that I had purchased. Though I had only gotten the sectional and tables delivered, the living room was already looking better. There were a few more things that were on back order, but they'd be delivered later in the week.

"It looks so much better in here," Me Me said, exiting the dining room. She had turned it into Santa's workshop. She had hundreds of gifts that she was wrapping daily.

"Don't it, though?"

"Yeah, got me waiting to buy something new for the house. Peanut gave me more money than I needed."

"Do it. It ain't yo' money." I laughed. "That's why I bought so much stuff. I can't wait 'til the rugs and pictures get here."

"Don't spend it all. We got a baby to prepare for."

"Oh, trust, I got the money for his room put up."

One of the delivery guys alerted me that they were finished, so we walked them to the door and threw a tip in for early delivery. Before they were in their trucks, Me Me said that she had to go. Peanut was on his way home and she wanted to meet him there. Since she made no mention of Sas, I figured that he hadn't found him yet. I was a little disappointed to say the least.

Yesterday, I finally got out the house. I went grocery shopping and picked up a few maternity outfits. I was tired of looking like a complete bum. After grabbing some fruit and a bottled water, I started toward the living room. I was so tired of being in that bed. Finally, I would be able to lounge on the sofa and watch television. Most importantly, I didn't have to go up and down the stairs to get something eat.

Just as I took my seat, the doorbell rang. I figured it was Me Me coming back to get some of the shit she had left in the middle of the floor. However, when I pulled the door open, all the air was knocked out of me. Em-kay stood there looking at me. For a second, I was like a deer in headlights. I didn't know if I should run and try to get my gun or what. We had a stare down then tears ran down his face.

"I'm sorry, Boo."

For some reason, I was still in shock. I couldn't move or say anything. It seemed like it had been forever since I had seen my brother. He looked good, too. A little heavier, but the weight looked good on him. Then, when I finally found words to say, Sas stepped from behind the post on the porch. That caused me to faint.

When I came to, I was lying across the sofa with a wet towel on my forehead. Sas was seated next to me and Em-kay was standing over me. I kept blinking my eyes over and over, to make sure that I wasn't seeing things. I couldn't believe that I was seeing them and together.

"W-W-Wha...H-H-How?" I stuttered. "W-Why?" Nothing was coming out the way it was lined up in my head.

"Shh," Sas hissed. "Calm down."

Immediately, I started crying. It felt so good to see him, but I didn't know how to react. I didn't know what was going on between him and Em-kay and I didn't want to set shit off. So badly, I wanted to wrap my limbs around Sas and never let go. I missed him like crazy. He must've read my mind because he pulled me up for a hug.

"What's going down?" he whispered in my ear. "You pregnant with my baby?"

"Yeah," I cried.

"What you cryin' for? Stop cryin'."

"I thought...I was never gon' see you again."

Sas hugged me for what seemed like forever, yet and still, I didn't want him to let me go. It had been four and a half hard, long months without him. For the longest, I thought he was gone forever, so seeing him had me all messed up in the head.

"What's up with you, though?" Sas questioned. "You ain't been eatin' or what?"

I shrugged. Though I had been eating good for a little over a week, it hadn't made up for the time I hadn't been eating. I knew because I looked at myself in the mirror every chance I got. I hated the way that I looked, and I was embarrassed for people to see me.

"Boo, you gotta take care of yo'self," Em-kay started. "You responsible for more than just yo' health. You got a baby to think about."

"I know. I've been eating and drinking a lot of water."

"Where you been, Boo?"

"For the last two months, here. It ain't like I had anywhere else to go."

"Yo' home is always yo' home, Purp. Always."

Finally, Em-kay took a seat and we all began to talk. Em-kay and Sas had worked through their differences and agreed to move forward. He gave his approval of Sas's and my relationship, which was all I ever wanted. I never wanted to come in between them, but I couldn't help what I wanted. And anything I wanted, I went after it, full speed. I hated that things happened the way that they did, but still, I was glad that it worked out.

Em-kay only hung around for a short time. Soon as he made his exit, I hopped right on Sas. Since I opened my eyes, I'd been fiending to do that. Placing my hands on the back of his head, I began to place kisses all over his face as he climbed the stairs with me.

"Damn, girl," Sas groaned. "You miss me or what?"

"You can't tell?"

"Yeah, a lil' bit."

"Where you been all this time?"

"Haiti," he answered, taking a seat on the bed. "Gettin' to know family. But I ain't tryna talk about that. I wanna talk about what's up with you."

"I don't wanna talk about me. You know what I wanna talk about?"

My arms were already around his neck, so I pulled him in closer and tongued him down. One of the things I missed the most, was kissing Sas. He had a pair of the softest lips. The way his tongue danced around mine stirred the butterflies in the pit of my stomach. Just thinking about how good he sexed me down the last time I saw him had me craving for that sensation. I wanted him to flip me over and give my body what it had been missing. However, one thought lingering in the back of my mind caused me to pause and pull back.

"You married, Sas?"

"What?" he asked, drawing his eyebrows together in a frown. "Who the fuck you been talkin' to?"

"Does it matter? Is they lyin'?"

"Yeah."

Him lying directly to my face, immediately pissed me off. I mean, we hadn't been in each other's presence two hours and he was already lying to me. I wasn't about to stand for that shit. I was setting the standards this time around.

"Smile."

"Why?" he questioned as his lips smiled faintly.

Boop! I punched his ass right in his fucking teeth. Simultaneously, he threw me off his lap onto the bed.

"The fuck you do that for?" he growled.

"'Cause, I wanted to hit you in that bitch ass tooth yo' ass lyin' through! Nigga, I got muhfuckin' proof! I saw the paper."

"Why you in my shit?"

"Uh-uh, don't try to turn this shit around on me," I said, grabbing a pillow and popping his ass in the back of the head with it.

Instantly, he jumped up from the bed and snatched me up by my shirt. I was so close to him, that I could literally feel his heart beating. Sas's eyes had darkened, so I knew that I had hit a nerve that I'd never touched on before. Out of all the times I should have been scared of him before, I was scared shitless. I couldn't read him; therefore, I couldn't tell if would hurt me or not. He had been gone for months, and there was no telling what he had been through, so I didn't know what he was capable of.

"For the last time," he finally spoke, "I'm gon' tell you. Don't put yo' fuckin' hands on me! I'll snap yo' fuckin' neck!"

Not knowing what Sas was thinking, I just kissed his ass. He still had his crease in his forehead and his eyebrows were still pressed together, but I didn't remove my lips from his. Finally, his grip loosened from my shirt. Though I was still mad, and the conversation wasn't dead, I felt the need to defuse the situation. I didn't know where Sas's head was, so I wasn't going to push my luck.

Next thing I knew, Sas had me folded like a pretzel with his head buried deep in my pussy. No lie, that nigga was giving me that head that Jodie gave Yvette in *Baby Boy*. Sas was sucking my pussy, sounding like he was sucking the last of his soft drink through a straw. Tears easily flow from my eyes, down to my ears as I reached my peak.

"Shit," I whined, sliding back. "Fuuck!"

"Bring that pussy back here!" He snatched me back by my thighs. "Sicka yo' ass."

Sas dove back in and ate my pussy merciless until I came two more times. He hadn't even delivered the dick yet and I was about to tap out. Once he eased inside, he began to work me over. He was dropping so much dick on me, that I was already cummin'.

"Mm, shit, baby," I moaned.

"Mm hmm," he hummed, working my ass. "Who makin' that pussy cum?"

"You are," I yelped as I climaxed. "Uuh!"

Never missing a beat, Sas continued stroking me. He wound his hips while pushing my thighs down to the bed. Then, he stood up in it and started dropping that big dick on me. Instantaneously, another nut was beginning to build.

"Oouu, shit," I whimpered, looking up at Sas.

"Mm hmm, I see ya eyes. You 'bout to go to heaven. It's alright."

"Oh, god! Oh, god!" I whined over and over.

"You see him? Wave at him. Tell him I sent yo' ass."

"Fuuck!"

A heat wave came over me then my body began to shake. My breathing was labored, causing me to feel high as fuck. Sas was dropping that dick off so good that I was still cummin'. Suddenly, I shook hard as fuck and my back lifted from the bed on its own. It felt like my soul lifted with it.

"Fuck, Sas!" I screamed from what I later found out was my first screaming orgasm.

"You like that dick?"

"Yes, baby," I breathed. "Yes."

He pulled out then flipped me over. I tooted my ass right up for him. He gripped my hips before ramming his dick inside me. I could tell that Sas was still mad at me and he was taking it out on my pussy. Sas wrapped his hand around my neck then pulled me up until my back touched his chest.

"If you wanna keep gettin' this dick, you betta learn how to act."

Still squeezing my neck, Sas was fucking the shit out of me while talking big shit. In between each sentence, he would use his free hand to smack my ass hard as hell.

"Keep disrespectin' me, and I'm gon' choke the life outta yo' ass." *Smack!* "Think I'm playin?" *Smack!* "Keep tryin' me and you gon' see, got dammit." *Smack!*

Although Sas was choking me, and I knew that he wasn't playing with my ass, I couldn't focus on the shit he was talking. My body was climaxing again. Sas released my neck just as I reached my peak. Immediately, I collapsed on the bed. Sas smacked me on my ass so hard that I jumped right back up.

"Bring that pussy back here!" he demanded. "I ain't fuckin' playin' wit'cho ass!"

I didn't know how much more of a beating my pussy or ass could take. Slowly, I assumed the position. Again, Sas rammed his big dick inside of me. Immediately, I flew back forward.

"Weak ass," Sas groaned as he laid on the bed next to me then tapped me to get on top. "Ride this dick and you bet not stop until I tell yo' ass to." I straddled him. "And you better ride it to the tip or I'ma knock yo' muhfuckin' ass out."

The last thing I wanted to do, was get knocked out by Sas. The way he was grilling me, I knew that he wasn't playing. He hadn't cracked a smiled since I popped his ass in his teeth. One thing was for sure, I had to ride his dick like it was a first-class flight. Hell, my life damned near depended on it.

15

SAS

Once again, **Purple** had me hotter than a six-alarm fire. It was like she thrived on pissing me off. The shit was like foreplay to her, but I wasn't playing those games. That was going to be the last time her fist met my teeth. After fucking Purple until she tapped out, I made her suck my dick until I came. I hated that I did, too, because it changed my mood. That good ass head caused me to be soft on her ass again. She was just an enigma that I just couldn't give up on.

The last thing I wanted was for Purple to find out that I was married. Hell, I didn't want anyone to know about it. That was why it was my best kept secret. Being in the country illegally, meant that I couldn't do shit. My plan was never to go back to Haiti, so I needed a home for myself in the U.S. So, on my 18th birthday, I married Trina. It was only for citizenship. She knew that as well and that was why she never tripped on anything I did. Also, that was why I kept her so close.

Honestly, I never thought about the fact that I was married. It was just a piece of paper that never crossed my mind after I signed the documents. However, since Purple had found them, I owed her an explanation. Only because our relationship had drastically changed.

"Purple," I started then looked down at her lying on my chest. "Shit ain't what it seems. Yeah, I'm married to Trina."

Purple's head popped up from my chest and I pushed it back down. Her body language told me that her mood had shifted. I wasn't trying to get her riled up. No matter how much I threatened Purple, I knew in the back of my mind that she would still turn up on me. I didn't want us battling on our first night back together, so I had to keep her calm.

"Listen," I continued. "It was only for citizenship. It wasn't no real shit. Yeah, I used to fuck with Trina, but she wasn't no different than any other bitch I fucked."

"And what the fuck makes me any different?"

"What you mean? You stayin' in my crib, you got the combo to the safe. I trust you. I didn't trust them other bitches like I trust you."

"So, you're only with me because you trust me?"

"I ain't say that was the only reason."

I knew females like the back of my hand. They needed verbal validation on what made them different than the other women you've been with. I wasn't into all that extra shit. Mainly because I never had to prove shit to a bitch. They all knew their places and we never had to discuss it. Once again, it was different with Purple. She had already claimed me as hers and now she was carrying my seed. Not to mention, I loved her silly ass. I had never loved a female before.

"What's the other reason?"

"Listen, I don't even wanna keep playin' games with you. I love you. You're the only female that I've ever loved. That's what separates you from any other hoe out there. A'ight? What we got is official." I placed my hand on the side of her stomach. "We a family. Always have been, always will be."

"She still got papers on you," Purple groaned, sitting up. "And I'on like that shit one bit. Sas, if something happened to you today, she'll get everything."

"Don't worry 'bout it. I'll handle it." I rubbed my hand over her little belly. "Damn, I can't believe we 'bout to have a baby."

She smiled. "A son."

I almost jumped out the bed when she said that. Though I couldn't see myself, I knew I was smiling from ear to ear. I could just feel my face stretched to the max.

"It's a boy?"

"Yeah." She giggled. "I found out the other day."

"That's what up."

The cell phone I had just purchased rang, so I knew that it had to be one of my boys. No one else had the new number yet. I grabbed it from my pants pocket and answered.

"Yo?"

"Nigga, I know you over there knee deep in the pussy, but come up out that shit for a minute," Peanut joked. "Meetin' at the shop in a hour."

"Bro, you tryna get me fucked up." I chuckled. "A'ight. Bet."

Purple was staring at me, so I knew that she had something to say. I sat there waiting to see if she was going to cut up or act like she had some sense.

"What is it?"

"I got to go meet up with the crew. We got some shit we gotta handle."

"Already? You just got home. They couldn't wait one day?"

"One day is like one year in this business. You already know how it goes. You ain't got no nine-to-five ass nigga. Ain't no time clocks being punched."

She hung her head. "I know. But damn."

"Ay, tighten up. Pick ya head up. Come on, come take a shower with me."

After fixing Purple's attitude in the shower, I picked out some fly shit to wear. It felt like forever since I had looked nice. I even threw on my jewels. By the time I exited the closet, Purple was already sleep. I strolled over in front of her, eased the cover back and kissed her stomach. I gave her a forehead kiss as I covered her back up. She inhaled deeply then exhaled hard.

"Ole ig'nant ass," I muttered then took a picture of her.

I ought to make her ass a meme: *How you sleep after startin' shit with yo' nigga and he put that dick on you.*

Hopping in my Challenger and hearing that engine roar, was like a welcome home present. It had been so long since I had ridden in some fly shit. In Haiti, I drove some shit that didn't even have a name to it. It got me to the few places I went, so I didn't give a damn about the rest. Besides, I didn't want nobody to know I had money. Before I left, I emptied two of my safes. The plan was to never come back, so I had more than enough money to live there comfortably for a while.

It was late, but I had to bend a few corners in the 'hood before heading over to the shop. I didn't stop to holler at anybody, I was going to wait until daylight to show my face. As I pulled up in front of the shop, Em-kay drove up behind me. We hopped out at the same time then met up between the cars. He dapped me up before passing a blunt to me.

"What's goin' down?" I spoke, taking a long drag of the blunt.

"We don' sat on our hands long enough. It's time to pop this shit off."

"I know, but damn. You coulda gave a nigga one day." I tilted my head. "It's been a minute."

"I feel ya. But that's my sister, so I'm gon' cock-block, my nigga."

Chuckling, I replied, "You ain't shit for that."

"How she doing, though?"

"She still crazy as fuck. That's for sure." I paused. "I'm havin' a son, man."

"Word?" He smiled. "Congrats, my nigga."

Nodding, I passed the blunt back. As I did, my eyes landed on a SUV that was parked up the street. I tapped Em on his chest then nodded toward the car.

"Who dat?"

"Shit if I know," Em replied, squinting his eye. "Let's go see."

Simultaneously, we pulled our guns from our waists then started toward the SUV. The engine started up then reversed up the street. Em and I stood in the middle of the road and looked at each other.

"What the fuck y'all been doin' since I left?" I inquired.

"I told you, DEA is on our asses."

"But this meetin' was planned just a hour ago, how they know to be here?" He shrugged. "Well, I just got my phone, so I know my line ain't tapped. Everybody need to dump they phone. Everything gotta start over. From the places we keep shit, to the cars we drive. We fuck around and need to get somewhere to stay for a minute. We don't know what these niggas got on us. Whateva it is, it ain't enough or they would've arrested us by now. So, we can't give 'em shit else to put on us."

"Fa sho'." He threw his arm around my neck and put me in a head lock. "It's good to have you back, bro," he said, rubbing his knuckles on the top of my head.

Laughing, I scooped him up and turned his ass a back flip to get him off me.

"Ahh!" he groaned. "Nigga, watch my damn shoulder."

"I don' told you to keep yo' hands to yo'self."

We laughed, dapped each other up again then started toward the shop. No lie, it felt good to have my brother back. It felt good to be back home. Even with the bullshit that was going on, everything still felt right. *Sas is back!*

16

PEANUT

"I know you don't call yo'self tryna check me," Me Me stated with her hand on her hip.

"I ain't tryna check you."

"OK, so why we talkin' 'bout the shit?"

"'Cause, I ain't got time to be dealin' with this drama shit."

"Like I got fuckin' time!"

"Why the hell you yellin'?"

"'Cause, you 'bout to piss me off talkin' 'bout the shit like I started it. That bitch pulled up on me! So, hell yeah, I beat her ass. Keep talkin' and I'ma beat yours."

"I ain't even tryna fight with you, Me."

"Well, shut the fuck up and put up the tree then, Pumpkin seed."

Me Me wasn't going to be satisfied until I pulled her damn lips off her face. Her lil' ass always had something smart to say. The only reason I hadn't knocked her ass upside the head for talking crazy to me, was because she was right. Ava and Vita had pulled up on Me Me. Ava knew that Me Me would dig in her shit, that was why she had Vita with her. Therefore, I couldn't be mad at Me Me. Still, I wanted to Gorilla Glue her fuckin' mouth closed.

After getting the Christmas tree up, I traveled up to the bedroom where Me Me was. She was loading up her overnight bag. I strode over to her and hugged her from behind.

"Why you always packin' yo' stuff up? Why you won't leave some stuff here?"

"Because I don't want my stuff all over the place."

"I don't like when you take all yo' stuff," I admitted, removing my arms from around her. "It makes me feel like you don't plan to come back or something."

"Don't I always come back? Ain't I always here when you get here? And ain't I always here when you wake up? Why you trippin' over some toiletries and the clothes I had on yesterday?"

"Whateva, man. I ain't even trippin'."

"Well, give me a kiss 'cause I'm 'bout to go."

I obliged then watched her strut away. I hated that shit, too. So badly, I wanted her to move in, but I wasn't going to keep pressing her about it. Due to her situation, I was giving her the time she asked for. However, a nigga didn't want to wait forever. I had given up all my hoes for Me Me, so she had to get with the program.

While getting dressed, I got a text on the burner phone from Em-kay with an address. He said to be there in an hour, so I drove right over. Somebody was watching us, and I wanted to circle the block a few times to check it out. The address was to a storage facility. Soon as I pulled up the gate began to open. Reef was standing on the opposite side, waving me forward.

"What's up, my nigga?" Reef dapped me up as I hopped out.

"Ain't shit. What's up with this?"

"I'on even know."

We traveled toward the office. Em-kay and Sas were already inside, blowing big smoke. I stood there confused because I didn't know what was going on. Sas passed me the blunt then Em-kay began to speak.

"I know y'all probably wonderin' why we here. It's simple. This is our new warehouse. The owners were about to shut this place down, and I took it off their hands. For now, the business is still registered to them. Only because I don't want to bring attention to us. This storage facility will house all our products. Coke, extra guns, money and cars."

Reef and I looked at each other briefly before turning back to Em-kay. I mean, I understood that we had to move shit, but I wasn't sure if putting it all in one basket was smart. However, Em and Sas were good at what they did, so I figured they had a plan.

While Em showed us around the place, he laid out the new plan. No one was to know about the storage facility, except for the four of us. Though Monty and Juke had been with the crew for a minute, Em didn't even want them knowing about it. We still hadn't found the drugs or who the CI was, so we were moving more careful than ever.

"The first floor is for the cars, the second floor is for cash and the third is where we'll keep the stash," Em-kay informed us, giving me and Reef keychains full of keys. "Every key on yo' chain is for yo' storage units only. You both got two company cars on the first floor. Use those cars for drops and pick-ups with Monty and Juke, and park it back in the storage unit. I don't want none of us touchin' nothing, so it's time to put the youngstas to work. Any word on the coke?"

"Nah," Reef replied. "Honestly, I don't think none of our people got it. Everybody been blowin' up my phone about the new shipment. They all need to re-up. Been needin' to."

"I got 100 keys downstairs. Since Bruce and Marlo bring in the most money, let them get first dibs. The shipment is coming in a few days, so we'll break everybody else off after."

"Nut, me and you gon' go chop it up with the youngins," Sas spoke. "Put them up on game."

Sas and I left the storage facility in his company Escalade with me driving. That nigga was sitting in the backseat like he was Frank Lucas or some shit. I didn't even fuck with him about it; I was just happy to have my nigga back. I was happy period because I was getting back to what I liked to do. When we pulled on the block in the east, all the niggas were eyeing the fuck out the ride. I pulled up alongside the curb next to Bad Dad, and Sas let down his window.

"Oh, shit!" Bad Dad boasted. "Sas, where the fuck you been at, my nigga?"

"Handlin' a lil' business, hop in the front seat."

Bad Dad jumped in the ride all smiles. He looked around the interior before turning back to face Sas.

"This shit bad ass, my nigga."

"'Preciate it. What's been going down, though?"

"Man, just tryin' not to be seen. Them people been over here fuckin' up the block. A nigga can't sell shit around here. They houndin' us over that murder shit. Y'all know they was DEA agents?"

"We do now. What happened, though?"

"Oh, you already know we stood tall. We did just like Peanut said and shut the fuck up. The next day, they let us all go. That one cracka was mad as fuck, too." He laughed. "He was pink as shit."

"Y'all niggas did good," Sas said, handing him a duffel bag that I knew was full of cash. "Make sure you take care of the 'hood. Where Dooney?"

"Up the block."

"Call him and tell him to come down. It's time to work. Y'all ready to work, right?"

"No doubt."

"Cool, 'cause I need y'all to get with Polo and Kells, so y'all can run y'all own crew. But I'ma have some other work for you and Dooney, too."

A few minutes later, Dooney hopped in the back with Sas, and we rode out. We went far north to a car dealership. Sas gave them the keys to their new rides and an address where they were to park the cars every night. They were now in charge of delivering dope and bringing the cash to Reef or myself. Everything was changing, I just hoped that it worked and kept them people off our asses.

On the way back to the storage, I swung by Ava's mama's house to see Kairo. As I approached the door, someone pulled it opened. It was Ava's oldest brother, Aaron.

"Why you let them hoes jump on my sister?"

"Man, shut the fuck up talkin' to me about some bitch shit. Where Kairo?"

"He ain't here," he said, placing his hand up as if it would stop me from going inside. "Now, get the fuck off my mama's porch."

"You need to jump off this bitch and get yo' shit together. Grown ass nigga still stayin' at home with his mama."

I turned to walk away, and the nigga stuck me from behind. Honestly, I had been waiting on some shit like that to happen, so I could have a reason to beat the dog shit out one of their asses. Ava was always talking shit; we were about to see if her brother was really about that life or not. As I was turning back to face him, the door slammed in my face. A nigga hitting me and running, was a bitch move. I wasn't about to let that shit ride. I remove my pistol, kicked the door in and unloaded in the damn house.

"Nut!" I heard Sas screaming. "Brang yo' ass on, nigga! What the fuck!"

When I turned back, Sas was jumping in the driver's seat. Instantly, I realized that I had lost my damn mind for a minute. Quickly, I ran to the SUV and hopped inside. Sas took off full speed.

"Nigga?"

"I know," I groaned. "Shit!"

"You gon' let them muthafuckas get you locked up. We already got heat on us."

"Fuck. I know. Shit."

Shooting Ava's mama's house up only meant more animosity between us. That was something that I did not need at the time. Especially since Ava had possession of Kairo. She was probably going to hold him hostage for a while. That was only going to make me angrier, which wouldn't be good for business. I had to find a way to suppress that shit before I got all our asses lock up.

17

ME ME

E ver since Peanut put that money in my hand, my ass had been on the go. Never in my life had I been tired of shopping, but buying for eight different people proved to be exhausting. Still, I wanted to make it the best Christmas ever, so I hadn't slowed down. That day, I decided to bring Chelle and Sasha along with me. I was tired of shopping alone; besides, I owed them for helping me beat Ava and her friend's ass.

"Ooh, thank you, bitch," Chelle sang, removing her designer bag soon as we got in the car. "I've been wanting one of these."

"Me, too," Sasha added. "See, you a real friend. Not like them bitches, Bree and Purple. They got a man and got ghost."

Sasha had no idea what had gone down with Purple and Bree. Of course, they were aware of Breelynn's condition and being on bedrest, but that was all they knew. I wasn't the type of friend that would tell someone your business even if they were friends also. I felt like, if someone wanted you to know something about them, they would tell you. Purple wanted no one to know anything about her, so I never even brought her up.

"Don't be like that," I replied. "They're your friends, too. You know Bree can't do too much. And Purple been vacationing with Sas."

"I just hope you don't change."

Peanut was my first real boyfriend, so I didn't know how being with him would affect my life. He was pressuring me to move in with him, and if I did, I was sure that some things would change.

"Who knows how things change when you move in with a nigga. None of us have been in their position. I just hope y'all don't be talkin' 'bout me behind my back if I move in with Peanut."

"I ain't hatin'," Chelle assured me. "We ain't single, so we can't kick it like single people no more. Sasha, you need to get you a man, then you'll understand why bitches ain't hanging on the block all day."

"Chelle, shut the fuck up. You and yo' nigga stay at home with y'all mama."

"And where your man stay?"

"Face deep in my pussy. Bitch, don't worry about it."

"A'ight, y'all," I interjected. "Don't even start. We had a good day."

Just as I said that, my cell rang through the car's Bluetooth. Bree was calling, so I picked up.

"Hey, girl."

"Hey, Me Me. What you doing?"

"Just got through shopping with Chelle and Sasha, on our way home."

"They in the car with you?"

"Yeah, you on the Bluetooth."

"Good, 'cause I'm planning a Christmas party. Well, it's more like a gathering. On the twenty-third, and I'm inviting everybody. Chelle, you and Sasha can bring a plus one if you want to. Wear ugly Christmas sweaters."

"OK," Chelle replied. "But what's up with you, though? We ain't seen you in a minute."

"I know. That's why I'm throwing this get together. We all ain't hung out in a minute and we need to catch up."

I looked in the backseat at Sasha. She was the main one talking shit about us kicking it, so I just had to see her face. Her ugly ass rolled her eyes, but I could tell that she was happy about the gathering. The call ended when we pulled up to the 'jects. With all the stuff I had in the car, I wasn't planning on getting out, but I did to check on my siblings.

When I stepped in the apartment, Erin was laying across the couch half sleep. Once she saw it was me, she woke all the way up. Her eyes traveled toward the kitchen. Just as I guided my eyes in that direction, I saw my mama coming out the kitchen. I hadn't seen her ass in over six months. I couldn't even see myself, but I knew that the look of disgust was all over my face. After all those months, she had the nerve to look at me with a smile on her face, rocking a big ass belly.

"Hey, daughter."

I just stood there looking at her as if she had shit on her face. I still couldn't believe that her ass had come back pregnant once again. At that point, I completely gave up. I wasn't going to continue to be a mama to my mama and all her kids while she kept having them.

"You ought to be ashamed of yo'self," I finally spoke. "You already got eight kids that you don't take care of, and you come in here carrying another one?"

"First of all, who the fuck you talkin' to?" my mama snapped. "This my shit, and I can bring however many kids I want to in this bitch."

"You know what?" I scoffed. "You sholl right. I hope you here to take care of 'em too 'cause I'm moving out."

Immediately, I stomped toward my room to pack my stuff. There was no way that I was hanging around to raise yet another baby. Hell nah! Soon as I snatched the closet opened, Erin strolled into the room.

"Me Me, don't leave. You already know she ain't gon' stay around long."

"Oh-fuckin'-well," I said, snatching my clothes out the closet. "I'm too young to be dealin' with this shit anyway. Peanut been askin' me to move in, so I'm gone."

"Me Me, what we gon' do?"

Quickly, I snapped my neck back and eyed her. Why was her

grown ass asking me about what they were going to do? Hell, she was older than me. Plus, she had a baby on the way. It was time for her to grow up as well, and neither her nor my mama would grow up if I continued to be their crutch.

"I don't know what the fuck y'all gon' do, Erin. You a grown ass woman, figure it out."

"Me Me," Derriyana called out with a smile on her face that slowly faded away. "Where you going?"

"This bitch moving," Erin stated as she made her exit.

"Moving?" Derriyana asked, strolling toward me. "Where?"

"With Peanut."

"Can I go with you?"

I grabbed the last of the clothes off the rack and threw them to the bed. Derriyana was looking at me for an answer, and I didn't want to break her little heart. Peanut said that it was cool for them to spend Christmas over and that was still going to happen, but I wasn't sure about living there. Besides, if I took my siblings, I still would be pacifying my mama.

"Look, Yana. I'll be back on Christmas Eve to pick y'all up. But I can't take you to live with me. Yo' mama is here, and she is going to take care of y'all. I'll still come by and make sure y'all got everything y'all need."

"I'm not doing what she say, Me Me."

"I don't care. As long as you're doing good in school, and not gettin' in trouble in the streets, I'll buy you everything you want. Deal?"

She mugged me for a minute then released a silly grin as she held her hand out.

"Deal."

I needed her to make that deal because I had spent too much on her for Christmas. And I had already purchased everything to redecorate her and Darla's room. Regardless of how I felt about my mama, I wasn't going to leave my siblings stuck out. I was getting nicer shit and so were they.

"Gone, bitch, leave," my mama stated as I walked into the living room with my first load of clothes.

"Shut the fuck up!" I spat. "Unfit, bitch. Keep yo' ass off drugs and take care of yo' muthafuckin' kids!"

"Who the fuck you think you talkin' to?" she said, raising up from the couch.

"You! And if you come close to me, I'm gon' slap the dust off yo' ass!"

She stood where she was and placed her hands on her hips.

"Get the fuck out!"

"You ain't gotta tell me, I'm already getting my shit."

I walked out the door then slammed it behind me. When I made it outside, Dre and his friends were leaning against the Range Rover. Once Dre saw me, he walked in my direction.

"Yo, Me Me, what's up?"

"What's up is, yo' mama is back and I'm moving out. Oh, and she brought along another baby."

"What? Aw, hell nah. Me Me, please take me with you. I don't want to stay here with her. She just gon' steal all our shit then leave."

"I can't take you right now, but I'll figure something out."

I didn't feel like going back and forth with him, so I told him what he needed to hear. Although I was still leaving, I felt bad about leaving my siblings behind. I had to shake that thought off me because it wasn't my issue. I wasn't obligated to care for them. Still, I was going to do it from afar. And I wasn't helping with any of the new babies. Precious was where I cut the cord.

Normally, I went by Purple's house to wrap gifts, but it was late by the time I got all my stuff loaded up. Then, I had to beg my siblings to let me leave. Well, more like bribed them. I gave them all $100 and told them that I would be back to pick them up in a few days. When I pulled into the garage, Peanut was already home. Since he was, I didn't bother grabbing anything out the car. I would just make him get it.

I was halfway up the stairs, when I heard Peanut cursing.

Opening the door to the bedroom, I saw him standing next to the dresser, holding his phone.

"Look, I'm not gon' keep arguin' with you over no dumb shit. I'on give a fuck about yo' mama house or yo' brother. Bring me my son, bitch!"

"Not until you apologize to my mama and my brother," I heard Ava say through the phone.

"Baby," I spoke, strolling toward him. "Hang up that phone, so I can suck yo' dick."

"You want me to bring my son over there and you got that bitch over there!" Ava shouted as I dropped Peanut's pants. "I told you I didn't want him around that bitch!"

"Man," Peanut groaned when I licked the tip of his dick. "Fuck you, a'ight? Bye." He hung up the line. "Shit, baby."

"You like that?" I asked then took all of him in my mouth.

"Fuck, yeah," he groaned. "That shit look sexy as fuck."

I was so damn frustrated, that I sucked his dick with no remorse. Next thing I knew, he was snatching his dick out and nutting on my breasts. Then, he returned the favor by giving me that awesome head only he knew how to give.

"Get ya ticket and climb yo' sexy ass on board," Peanut said, directing me to get on top of him. "Ride this dick into the sunset."

"Mm," I moaned as I eased down on him. "Ss."

"Shit, that pussy wet," he groaned. "Ride that shit to the tip."

Slowly, I bounced up and down his pipe making sure to ride it to the tip as he requested. Peanut was biting his bottom lip while gazing up at me. He looked sexy as fuck to me. I still couldn't believe that he was mine, and I was going to do everything to ensure that he stayed just that. I rode the shit out his dick until I felt my climax building.

"Mm, shit," I moaned. "I'm 'bout to cum."

"Damn," he grunted. "You gon' make me cum, too. Ride that shit. Don't stop."

I wasn't going to stop because my nut was near. However, in the back of my mind, I was more worried about his nut. We weren't using protection and I wasn't on any birth control. The last thing I wanted to be, was pregnant with my mama and my sister. That was some ghetto shit.

"Oouu, fuck," I whimpered, reaching my peak. "You cummin', baby?"

"Ahh, shiit," he groaned.

I tried to hop off his dick, but he pulled me back down.

"I said, don't stop!"

"Baby," I whined as he gripped my waist.

"Shit," he groaned then flipped us over. "You gon' be my wife, and you gon' have my baby."

"OK, baby," I moaned when he started back stroking me. "Ooh, that feels so good."

"Mm hmm, I know. But you got the best pussy ever."

He leaned in to kiss me and I wrapped all my limbs around him. Peanut didn't even realize that his ass was about to be stuck with me. I wasn't playing that shit like he played with Ava. She was all talk, but I'd beat Peanut's ass if he tried to play me. However, he had mentioned being his wife on more than one occasion, so I was going to give him a chance to prove himself.

18

EM-KAY

"Damn, that ass fat," I joked, smacking Bree on the ass when I entered the closet. "Where you get that ass from, girl?"

She giggled. "My husband put it on me."

"Damn right." I hugged her from behind, securing my arms around her stomach. "What you wearin'?"

It had been a minute since I had taken Bree out on a date; therefore, I was taking her out for a romantic evening. Since I'd come back from Haiti, I had been busy running around to change up my operation. Bree promised to be understanding of it, and she was, so I was going to show her my appreciation. Not to mention, we only had a short amount of time to ourselves.

"I don't know. I think I'ma wear this red dress you got me, since red yo' favorite color."

I laughed. "Oh, you tryna get lucky?"

Before Bree could respond, the doorbell rang. I wasn't expecting anybody, so I grabbed my piece from the dresser before going downstairs. As I made my way down, I could see Reef's ride parked in the driveway. Something had to be going on for him to pop up on me.

"What's goin' down?" I asked, dapping him up.

He stepped inside then looked at me.

"Bro, why the keys back in the warehouse?"

"Huh?" I frowned. "What you mean they back in the warehouse?"

"Nigga, I went to meet the delivery dudes that was dropping off the stuff for the nail shop. I walk inside, they stacked up in the middle of the damn floor."

Instantly, a nigga started feeling like somebody was fucking with me. Why the hell would they take the shit just to bring it back? That shit didn't make no sense to me.

"Man, who the hell fuckin' with us?" I groaned. "Nut 'nem didn't find out nothing?"

"Ain't none of them niggas hit me."

I was ready to jump into action, but I looked back and saw Bree standing at the top of the stairs. There was no way that I could disappoint her after she had been so patient.

"Get up with them niggas and have everybody meet at the W hotel tomorrow at noon."

"Bet." He dapped me up again. "What's up, Bree?"

"Hey, Reef," she replied, then he made his exit.

Bree was looking at me with questioning eyes but I didn't speak a word to her. I just went back up to the room and got ready for our date night.

During date night, my mind was on the drugs. Honestly, I wanted to go move that shit out the warehouse. At the same time, I didn't want to touch it. I didn't know who had taken the drugs, or for what reason. For all I knew, the shit could be tainted somehow. Or it could be some flour. Who knew what the fuck was in the middle of that floor? Yet and still, I needed to find out who was fucking with me. We hadn't made any enemies or stepped on any toes. Maybe we had gotten close and they felt the need to put the shit back. Whatever the reason was, I had to get to the bottom of it and soon.

"What's wrong, baby?" Bree inquired. "You've been quiet all night."

"I just got a lot on my mind. Nothing I want to worry you with."

"You already know if something is bothering you it bothers me, so tell me what's up."

"The shit that was stole...they brought it back." Bree frowned hard. "I know. That was my reaction. I'on know what the fuck going on."

"I don't know but you need to get it out of there asap. Especially with folks running in and out of there."

Nodding, I replied, "I know. That's what I've been thinkin' 'bout. I don't know who watchin' the spot and I ain't tryna get nobody caught up. I gotta move it though, I can't risk it. But enough about that shit. We on a date. We 'pose to be talkin' 'bout us."

"You're right. Just know that I'm here to help wheneva you need me." She winked. "Anyway, I know you busy and all, but I need you to put the tree up. How I'm gon' host a Christmas party for our friends with no Christmas decorations?"

"Them niggas ain't used to no Christmas no way. Long as we got food and liquor, everything else don't really matter. And don't spend too much on gifts neither. I ain't them niggas' daddy."

"You so cheap." Bree giggled. "I got you, baby."

Once the food came to the table, our conversation was cut short. Bree and I both loved food, so we didn't play when it came time to eat. For some reason, watching Bree eat made me think about Purple. I had only seen her once, but it was obvious to me that she wasn't eating good. I knew that it had a lot to do with what she was going through, and I felt bad. Mainly, because I was the reason for her heartache. Though we weren't beefing, I had to make shit right with her. Especially since I had made things completely right with Sas.

"You talk to Purp?" I asked. "Did she say she was comin' through?"

Bree smiled. "Yes, she's coming...You haven't talked to her?"

Slowly shaking my head, I responded, "Nah. Not since we came back. I don't even know what to say to her. I ain't even gon' lie " I paused briefly. "Seein' her pregnant made me feel some type of way. I mean, I knew that she was pregnant, but seein' her was different. And I feel bad 'bout that shit 'cause I celebrated with Sas. That's fucked up, ain't it?"

"Hell yeah, it is." Her eyes went from mine, down at her stomach then back up at me. "You can't be like that, Em. You can't have that double standard. Me and her are one and the same."

"You right. I know the way I think is fucked up, that's why I always ask you. Man, I'm glad you stayed down. I don't know what I'd do without you."

"Luckily, you won't ever have to find out."

I chuckled but cut it off when I saw Estelle strutting toward us. I hadn't seen or talked to her since she had me jump out her plane, so I was confused on why she was coming to see me. One thing was for sure, seeing her didn't mean good news.

"Hello," Estelle spoke.

Bree looked at me sideways as I stood up to speak and allowed her to take a seat. I gave her a wink and a nod to let her know to be cool. Estelle was a nice-looking woman, so anything could be running through Bree's mind. I didn't want nothing to pop off because I knew that Estelle's men were close by.

"Good evenin'," I spoke, taking my seat. "I'm surprised to see you. What brings you out?"

"I was in the neighborhood." She smiled. "Aren't you gonna introduce us?"

"Yeah, this is my wife, Breelynn. Bree, this is Estelle."

Bree gave me that 'oh' look then reached her hand out to shake Estelle's.

"Nice to meet you, Estelle."

Confused, I sat there quietly. Estelle didn't even stay in the states, so I knew her reason for popping up was one other than the reason she had given me. Already knowing the game, I sat waiting for her to speak.

"I hear you're having a little problem," Estelle finally spoke.

"I do, but it's being handled."

Not sure which problem she was referring to, I wasn't going to mention either. A true player never showed his hand.

"So, you found out who's responsible?"

"My team is handlin' it."

Estelle smiled then gave me a look. Sort of like the look your parent gave you when they knew that you weren't telling the truth. Technically, I was telling the truth. My crew was handling business, I just wasn't sure which problem she was mentioning.

"You know, Em-kay, I gave you the benefit of the doubt that you could handle Dallas. Now, I'm not so sure. Don't get me wrong, I appreciate you getting my money to me on time. Nonetheless, if someone is able to get into your warehouse and take from you, I don't know how comfortable I am with sending you packages."

"Like I said, it's being handled. We got the bricks back."

She raised her eyebrows. "Did you?"

Something told me that Estelle knew everything, so there was no need to keep bullshitting with her. If she thought that I was a liar, she probably wouldn't want to do business with me anymore. That was something that I could not let happen.

"Straight up," I started. "Someone took a few bricks and brought 'em back. We don't know who took them. But I promise you, we won't stop lookin' until we find that muthafucka."

"Perfect, because I want you to bring that person to me. You got one week or I'm going to find a new distributor."

Estelle stood up from the table then sashayed away slowly. Bree and I both watched her until she made her exit. Simultaneously, we looked at each other. I was lost for words and I guess Bree was, too. So, like the fat muthafuckas that we were, we started back eating. Honestly, if Estelle got someone else to push her coke, I wouldn't even give a fuck. I had made and saved more than enough money to do whatever I wanted to do. I had two businesses opening in a few months, so I was set. Truthfully, she would be doing me a favor. Her threats weren't bothering me, yet and still, I was going to find out who was fucking with me. I wasn't letting that shit ride, no matter how long it took to find them.

19

BREELYNN

Though Em-kay was playing it cool, the pop-up visit from Estelle had me worried. She threatened to stop his supply, but something told me that it would be more than that. I didn't know much about the dope game; however, I knew that the plugs didn't mess around. I wasn't physically capable of helping Em-kay, yet, I was going to do everything I could to prevent something from happening to him. My only problem was, I had no idea what to do. Estelle wanted the thief, and if Sas and Peanut couldn't find out who it was, I damned sure couldn't. Still, I felt like I had to do something.

Since I wasn't capable of handling stuff on my own, I phoned Purple and Me Me. Their men were deep in the game, and I was sure that they had their backs just like I had Em's. Between the three of us, I knew that we could come up with something that would help them. If we didn't, we definitely had to be prepared to stand beside them if a war broke out.

"What's up, girl?" Me Me spoke, taking a seat on the sofa. "What you call us over here for?"

Purple was looking around the house as if it was unfamiliar to her. It probably felt funny for her to be back in the house after all those months. Especially after the exit she made.

"Because, some shit is going on and we gotta have the guys' backs."

"Shit, like what?" Purple inquired, still looking around.

"The plug walked up on me and Em last night while we were on a date. She said that if they didn't bring her the people responsible for stealing the drugs out the warehouse, she was cutting Em-kay off."

"So?"

"So? So, when have you ever known for a plug to just cut someone off and let them go freely? Em has seen this lady. I've seen this lady. You really think she gon' let us walk without consequences?"

"Sounds like a personal problem to me," Purple mumbled sarcastically.

"So is the situation with Trina, but I agreed to help you when the time comes."

"Trina, who?" Me Me asked. "What's going on?"

Purple stared at me with her lips pressed together. I stared back with one of my eyebrows raised. I wasn't going to say shit, I just wanted to remind her that she needed help just like I did.

"I might as well tell you. Bree ole talkin' ass," Purple groaned. "Sas is married to Trina."

"Hood Trina?" Me Me frowned. "What the fuck?"

"Exactly. But we ain't here to talk about my situation. Bree, what are you askin'?"

"Honestly, I don't know. But what I do know is I don't want Em-kay dead or in jail. I would hope that you two want the same. Especially you, Purple."

"Of course, I want Sas home, but he don't tell me nothing about the game. We don't even talk about his role."

"Peanut either," Me Me added. "How we gon' help them?"

I didn't have an answer for them. All I knew, was when the shit hit the fan, I wanted Em-kay to come out alive and free. And being that Em-kay was the leader of his crew, I had to step up and make sure us women held them down.

"Bree, I hear what you sayin'," Me Me continued. "But I ain't sure how we can help them."

"I ain't either, I just know we got to keep their backs covered at all times. Purple, I already know you got a gun, but do you, Me Me?"

She shook her head, so I reached over and pulled one from my bag. I had three guns, so I was giving her one to hold.

"Look, I don't know how all this shit gon' play out. But I know what I signed up for. We gotta be ready in case the plug acts up, in case a war starts behind the drugs gettin' stole from the warehouse, or if the DEA comes back askin' questions. We gotta stay physically and mentally ready at all times."

"Bitch, I ain't new to this shit," Purple expressed. "Ask for a lawyer and don't say shit else. Not one word. And as far as that other shit, I ain't worried about it. I keep my shit on me."

"Crazy ass." Me Me laughed. "Don't be poppin' off, shootin' at people, bringin' attention to us."

"I ain't. Shit, my pregnant ass can't do nothing. Besides, Sas said if I act up, he ain't gon' give me no dick." Purple laughed. "So, you already know a bitch been walkin' around on mute, since I can't control my mouth."

We all laughed then Me Me asked Purple about Sas being married. She went ahead and told her about it while they helped me decorate the tree that Em-kay must've put up before he left that morning. The entire time, Me Me was trying to talk Purple out of killing Trina. She knew Purple just like I knew her, so she already knew once Purple's mind was set, there was no going back. The only thing that would prevent her from offing Trina, was a divorce.

"Y'all know, Chelle and Sasha feel some type of way since y'all ain't been around," Me Me casually mentioned as we began to clean up the mess.

"I invited them to the party."

"Yeah, but y'all ain't been around in a minute. I just told them that you was still on bedrest, and I told them Purple been on vacation with Sas. Chelle ain't really trippin', it's Sasha ass hatin' as usual. But in her defense, it's been like five months since y'all been around."

"I do miss them," Purple admitted. "We all haven't kicked it in a while. I guess the party will be a lil' reunion. Sasha's ass bet not flirt with Sas, though. That's all I know."

Of course, Me Me and I had to laugh at that. Sasha was always flirting with Sas, so there was no telling what would happen at the party. For Sasha's sake, I hoped that she didn't flirt with Sas. We had enough going on already, there was no need for us to be beefing with each other.

"We're gonna have fun," I assured them. "No drama. All love."

"I hope so," Me Me breathed. "I'm dealin' with enough drama."

"That bitch Ava still trippin'?" Purple inquired.

"Not only her. My mama showed up out of nowhere...talkin' shit...and pregnant again."

The look of shock had to be all over my face because that was exactly what I was. Faye's ass was always pregnant, so I shouldn't have been surprised. However, I was. Purple's ass found it to be comical.

"What's in the water, chile?" Purple giggled.

I laughed. "Good dick."

"I guess so." Me Me shrugged. "Erin's ass is pregnant, too. Peanut wants me to have his baby, and my dumb ass said 'OK.' I ain't even sure if I'm ready for all that yet. I wanted to finish school before I had a baby."

"You might as well be miserable with us." Purple laughed then the doorbell rang.

I wasn't expecting anyone, so all three of us traveled to the door. When I pulled the door open, my brother, Rocco, was standing there with my grandmother. My grandmother looked upset and Rocco looked sad, so I didn't know what was going on.

"Here. Take him," my grandmother stated, pushing Rocco toward me. "He don't obey my rules. He's smokin' that dope."

Rocco started snickering, pissing our grandmother off even more. Honestly, I had to keep from laughing myself. The smell of weed was coming off Rocco, so I knew that was what my grandmother was calling dope.

"See." My grandmother huffed. "I can't deal with him. I went by Crystal's, nobody was there. Have you talked to her?"

"Um, excuse me," Me Me interjected. "Bree, I'm 'bout to run, but I'll call you later."

Purple was right behind her. After speaking to my grandmother and Rocco, Purple and Me Me took off. Just like Purple's, Rocco and my grandmother's eyes roamed around the house. They had never been over before, so I took a seat on the sofa while they checked the place out.

"This is a nice house, Bree," my grandmother stated, taking a seat next to me. "I'm scared to even ask what Em-kay does for a living."

"Don't. Just tell me what's going on."

"You gon' have to deal with Rocco. He don't listen to shit I say. I told him about coming in my house at all times of the night and he's still sneakin' in and out. And he's smoking that dope. I'm too old to be dealing with him. He raises my pressure up, Bree. Have you talked to Crystal? I've been by that house all week and nobody's been there."

"Honestly, I haven't talked to her since I left."

My grandmother still didn't know about my mama's addiction, and I still couldn't bring myself to tell her about it. Especially not after Rocco had been giving her a hard time.

"Well, I don't know what's been going on with y'all, but whatever it is, y'all need to get it together. There's no way that you and Crystal should go months without talking. And Rocco needs discipline. And where is Brendyn?"

"Still in jail. He violated his probation, so he gotta do 28 months."

"Bree!" Rocco called out, interrupting the conversation. "Ay, y'all got some ketchup up in here?" he inquired, holding a loaf of bread.

"Look in the pantry by the stove." I looked back at my grandmother and she was shaking her head. "You want something to eat or drink, Grandmother?"

"No, baby, I'm OK."

"I know he's rough around the edges, but Rocco's a good kid. I ain't in the best position to be dealing with him, but I'll talk to Em-kay about him staying for a while."

"I understand that. And believe me, I don't want to add to your stress, but I'm too old to be dealing with Rocco's hard head. I don't know what's going on with Crystal, but I'm gon' find out."

"Man, what the hell is you doing in my kitchen makin' sandwiches and shit?" I heard Em-kay ask.

He had gotten home just in time. I didn't want to engage in a conversation about my mama, and Em-kay could deal with Rocco. A few seconds later, Em-kay strolled into the living room.

"Hey, Ms. Lady," Em-kay spoke, leaning over to hug my grandmother. "What's going on?"

Sighing, my grandmother replied, "I need y'all to take Rocco off my hands until I can catch up with Crystal."

Em-kay kissed my forehead before taking a seat next to me.

"That ain't a problem," Em-kay assured her, while looking at me. "He's family, he's welcomed."

"You sure? 'Cause I don't wanna put y'all out. I know y'all are newlyweds and preparing for the baby, but I need a break."

"It's cool, Ms. Turner, he can stay."

I wasn't sure how everything was going to work out, but I was going to leave that up to Em-kay since he was the one that agreed without hesitation. I wasn't about to worry myself about Rocco. Being around Em-kay was what he wanted anyway. I just hoped that Em kept him out his bullshit. I didn't need to be worried about both of them.

After eating dinner and getting Rocco settled, Em-kay and I took a shower and got ready for bed. Honestly, I was surprised that he was home so early. With everything that was going on, I didn't expect him until later.

"How was your day?" I asked, taking a seat on the bed.

"It was pretty easy. We got the stuff checked and moved out the warehouse which was most important."

"What about the other thing?"

"What I tell you about worrying about the business? Me and the crew can handle it. I don't want you worrying 'bout nothing but getting our son here healthy. I don't even want you worryin' 'bout Rocco, I got him."

"Bae, please don't have him in no shit."

"Listen," Em-kay stated, taking a seat next to me on the bed. "I ain't tryna get him caught up. Trust me, that's the last thing I want. But if he don't wanna go to school and make something of himself, he gotta find a hustle. He can't chill around here all day every day. He wanna be a man, he gotta learn how to stand on his own two, feel me?"

"I hear you, but I don't want him on the block, dealin' drugs."

"Well, talk to him and see what he wanna do, and get back to me."

"OK." I reached over and rubbed my hand down his chest. "Now, can I have some you time? You been actin' stingy with the meat all week. I'm in need of a fix."

"Yo' ass stay horny."

"Yeah, 'cause you stay rationing the dick. Ain't nothing gon' happen to the baby. I'm 31 weeks, so if he does come, he'll have a good chance of surviving."

Em-kay just looked at me, so I took it upon myself to straddle him. When I wanted dick, I damned near had to rape him. I understood and respected the fact that he was worried about our munchkin, but mama needed some sexual healing. If he wanted me to not worry about his business, then he needed to keep me full of dick. Otherwise, I had nothing but time to worry about it.

"Gon' and take it," Em-kay said as he laid back. "I like it better when you take it anyway."

He hadn't said nothing but a word because I was going to take it anyway. Now that I knew he liked it, my ass was going to become Bill Cosby. Every time I saw him, I was going to be on his ass like flies to shit. He just didn't know, he had created a monster well, more like a sex demon.

20

PURPLE

Just as I hopped in my ride, Em-kay was pulling into the driveway. I hadn't seen him since he showed up with Sas, so when he waved me down, I waited for him to get out the car. I didn't know why, but seeing my brother still gave me anxiety. I mean, I knew that we were cool and all, yet and still, I felt uneasy around him. It was as if I was waiting on him to retaliate.

"What's going down, Boo?" he asked then leaned in the window to kiss my cheek. "You a'ight?"

"Yeah, I'm good. You?"

"Yeah, I'm straight. You lookin' better. How's my nephew doing?"

"I feel better. He's good...keepin' me hungry."

Em-kay chuckled. "Yeah, yo' nephew keep me and Bree eatin'. Yo, I ain't wanna hold you up, I just wanted to speak. We ain't really had a chance to chop it up for real. Let's meet up for lunch or something tomorrow. I wanna talk to you about a few things."

"OK. Just text me where and what time."

As I watched Em-kay stroll toward the house, an instant calm came over me. For a while, I felt like he would try to get even with me for shooting him, now I felt as if things were going to work out fine. Besides, he had too many other things to worry about than me.

When I pulled up to the house and saw that Sas was home, I was sort of surprised. Not really, because Em-kay had made it home early, but I still wasn't expecting Sas to be in the house. Stepping into the house, the smell of cooked food invaded my nostrils. I let my nose lead me toward the smell.

"Welcome home, baby," Sas spoke with a smile.

Sas was standing by the bar, looking good as fuck. He had gotten his hair cut and goatee shaped up; I wanted to lick the shit out his face. I looked toward the kitchen, and a chef was standing in front of the stove.

"What you got going?"

"Well, I realized we ain't never been on a date, so we doing the date thang. Gone upstairs and get ready."

I blushed so hard that I almost chuckled. Sas wasn't the romantic type, so for him to plan a date, meant the world. After kissing his cheek, I hurried up the stairs. A purple dress was laid out across the bed with a shoe box and three small boxes next to it. One by one, I opened the smaller boxes. Sas had gotten me a matching gold neck-lace, bracelet and earring set. Quickly, I hopped in the shower to freshen up.

As I made my way back down the stairs, the lights were dim and soft music was playing in the background. I couldn't stop smiling for nothing. All I ever wanted was Sas, so anything he did to make me feel special, was a bonus. I knew what type of dude he was; there-fore, I wasn't expecting romantic dinners. I just expected Sas to be Sas.

"Damn, you look good," Sas complimented, taking my hand. "I see you tryna get ya weight up."

I giggled. "I got my man back, so I'm feelin' a lot better."

Releasing a little smirk, Sas led me to the dining room. It was a good thing that I had bought furniture for it; otherwise, we'd be eating in the bed like we used to. After taking our seats, the chef came in with drinks and appetizers. The entire time, a smile was on my face.

"What's up with you?" Sas inquired. "You surprised?"

"Hell yeah." I blushed. "I never would've expected something like this from you."

"Why, 'cause I'ma street nigga? We know how to treat a female we like."

"You like me?"

"No." He eyed me. "I love ya."

Cheesing hard as fuck, I replied, "I love you, too."

"I know."

"Yo' cocky ass makes me sick." I chuckled. "I missed you so much, though. Like, you have no idea. Don't ever leave me again."

"You sayin' you wanna be with me forever?"

"Sas, I'm a teenager that's been in love with you for years, and I'm pregnant with yo' baby. Of course, I'ma say I wanna be with you forever."

"But will you mean it?"

"Are you tryna ask me something?"

"I ain't tryna ask you shit. I'm askin' you what I wanna know."

Rude bastard!

"Sas, I shot at Em behind you. How can you not think I mean it? I'm in love with you. Yes, I want us to be together forever and raise our son."

He sat there quiet, so I began to eat the eggrolls. I didn't know what was up with Sas and his line of questions, but I wasn't going to let it make me forget about all the food that was in front of me.

"You know I ain't into feelins and emotions and shit. I don't know how to deal with the shit, but I'ma try. We gotta stop arguin' and fightin', though. I don't wanna bring our son up around that. We love each other, so ain't no reason for us to be fightin' like we do. I know I got business to handle. And trust me, I will handle that shit. For now, I just need you to chill. Don't make shit harder than it gotta be."

Honestly, I had been doing a good job of that. Ever since the fight, I'd been on my best behavior. Therefore, I didn't know why he was making a speech. Yet and still, I didn't comment on it, I just continued to eat. That was the only way to keep the reckless shit I was thinking inside my head.

"You hear me, Purp?"

"Yes. I hear you."

Before he could reply, the chef entered with the main course. The food was so damn good, that Sas could make any demand he wanted, and I would agree to it. All I wanted to do was eat that good ass food; I didn't care about nothing else. Sas could talk all the shit he wanted to, but the fact that he was married to that bitch, was always on my mind. No matter how much I loved Sas and wasn't going to leave him, yet, I was still a little bitter about it. Though I hadn't voiced my opinion about it since the night I punched his ass, I hadn't let it go. My focus had just been on gaining weight and getting healthy, instead of digging in his shit every second of the day.

I was stuffed but when the chef brought out the chocolate-cherry mousse, I couldn't help myself. Sas just sat there watching me stuff my face. He looked as if he was full as fuck and surprised that I was still going.

"What?" I asked, licking my spoon.

"Nothing. I'm just watchin' you feed my son. Enjoyin' the fact that yo' mouth movin', but ain't no slick shit comin' out of it."

"You better leave me alone before I get started."

"Bet." He chuckled, standing up from the table. "Let me go pay dude and get him outta here."

I finished my mousse then ate Sas's while I waited for his return. My ass was stuffed, but I couldn't seem to stop eating. When Sas came back, he shook his head at me before taking my hand. He led me up to the bedroom then out on the balcony that surrounded it. Mini Tiki torches lit the balcony and rose petals covered the ground. To most it wasn't anything to coo over, but knowing how Sas was, it felt like the perfect date. I knew that it took everything in him to plan something to make me feel special, because he wasn't the type.

Sas took his seat in one of the lounge chairs and I sat on his lap. He grabbed the blunt that was on the table and fired it up. It had been so long since I had smoked, and the smell of the bud took me back to when I used to chill on the block with my girls. Being pregnant was boring as fuck.

"Blow the smoke in my face," I suggested.

"Nah, we ain't fuckin' this kid up. It's bad enough you starved his ass for four months."

"It's not fair that you get to have all the fun. I'm tired of being bored."

"You act like if you smell this smoke that a damn party gon' break out. If you bored, do what other pregnant women do, shop for the baby. Hell, you can shop for yo'self 'cause yo' side of the closet is skimpy as fuck, and I'm sicka you in my shit. All my damn shirts stretched out in the tittie part."

I chuckled. "Sound like you need to go shoppin', not me."

"Since we already sharin' shit, we may as well gone and get married."

I started to chuckle again, but I saw the serious look on his face. It took me more than a few seconds to think of a response that wouldn't start some shit. How the hell did he think that we were going to get married and his ass was already married?

"Did you forget that you are already married to that "

"The fuck that got to do with what I just asked you?"

"You ain't ask me shit, Sas. You made a suggestion."

"So, you wanna get married or what, man?"

"If that's how you askin', hell no," I said, standing from his lap. "And the next time you think about askin' me, you bet' not be married to that bitch."

I turned and made my way back into the bedroom. Truthfully, I wanted to kick my own self in the ass for not being able to hold my tongue, but I still couldn't help myself. Especially not after that half ass proposal. That nigga didn't even present me with a ring. I was probably going to end up on the 'no dick' list; however, I didn't give a damn. I was going to put him on the list, too. Long as he was married to that bitch, *his* ass wasn't going to get none.

As I sashayed into the brunch spot that Em-kay and I used to visit once a month, I saw that he was already seated. Em-kay had never been punctual for anything, except business, so I was surprised that he was there. It made me wonder if our breakfast was personal or business.

"What's goin' on, Boo?" Em-kay spoke, standing up to hug me.

"Life." I chuckled then took my seat.

"Facts. Life is going on."

I sat there staring at Em-kay, wondering what was going on in his head. He seemed to have a lot on his mind. When it came to me, Em-kay was never short with his words. However, since the first time I'd seen him, he'd been short.

"What going on, bro?" I inquired. "What's on ya mind? I mean, I know we ain't kicked it in a minute, but I know when something is bothering you."

Before he could answer, the waiter strolled up with our food. I always got the shrimp and grits, so he ordered it for me. Once I started eating, I forgot all about the question I asked.

"So," Em-kay stated. "Yesterday, I was tryna place an order for supplies for the nail shop and the card was declined. I check the account and find out you withdrew the money."

"I guess it was a shock to you just like it was when I went to the bank and found out about the account. How could you have an account for me and not tell me? Furthermore, why were you being so cheap with me with all that money in the account?"

"Because it had a purpose. I told you that I was going to get you a business. That's what it was for. What you do with the money?"

"I lived off it. It was my money, right? From a life insurance policy from Granny."

"Technically, yeah, but I've made deposits, too. I had plans for the money. Plans to set you up for the future. And now that you, um..."

"Now that I'm what?"

"Startin' a family."

Taking a second to look at Em-kay, I began to read him. He looked so uncomfortable, but I didn't know what had him that way. Em-kay was always so confident; therefore, I didn't know what was going on with him.

"Be real with me, Em. What's wrong?"

He sighed. "I'm just tryna get used to the fact that you pregnant, a'ight? I just...you my lil' Boo...and I can't believe you 'bout to have a baby."

I took a sip of my water before speaking. "Do you feel the same way about Sas having a baby, or is it just me?"

"Truth moment...just you." I smacked my lips. "I know, Boo. I know it's selfish for me to feel that way. And I'm workin' to try to move past it. I know you love Sas and whether he said it to you or not, 'cause I know he a asshole, I know he loves you too. I'll never in life say it again, and I'll deny it if you ever said I admitted it, but Sas is probably the only guy you could have fallen for that I would accept. Not just 'cause he's my best friend, 'cause I know he can take care of and protect you that same way I would. True, I'm still tryna get used to you and that big belly, but I accept y'all's relationship, and the fact that you pregnant. A'ight?"

"OK." I sat quiet briefly. "Did you know that Sas is married to Trina?"

"What?" He frowned. "Fuck you talkin' 'bout he married Trina?"

"I see you didn't know either."

While we finished our food, I told Em-kay about how I found the license, and what Sas had told me. Em-kay was oblivious to it all. I could tell by the way he was looking at me, that he was going to question Sas about it. Sas was probably going to be pissed at me, but I didn't care. Honestly, I still had animosity in my heart about it. I felt as if I had been tricked into committing adultery.

"Then he had the nerve to half ass propose to me last night. Bastard didn't even have a ring."

Em-kay started laughing. "You know my bro don't know shit about that. It's sad to say, but the fact that he even asked, is as good as it's gon' get. What you say?"

"I said 'hell, nah.' How could I say 'yes,' and he's married to someone else?"

"But you know it's all bullshit. You know how Sas is, so either you gon' be with him or you ain't. Either give him time to handle that situation or move on. Ain't no sense of stayin' together to fight about it. Either you all in or you ain't, Boo."

Em-kay put a lot on my brain to think about. I loved Sas more than anything, but I didn't like our situation. My plan was to get rid of Trina; however, Em-kay had me thinking about giving Sas time to fix it. My patience was thin, though, and I wanted shit done expeditiously. But doing shit my way, was what fucked everything up in the first place, so maybe I should let Sas handle it. *Nah, I ain't letting shit go until I see divorce papers!* He had five months and the clock was ticking.

21

SAS

After the romantic date I planned for Purple failed, I knew that I had to put some action behind my words. With trying to keep the business intact and getting back in the groove of things, I hadn't had a chance to talk to Trina about getting a divorce. I needed to get up with her soon because Purple was tripping. Once she ended our date by making a grand exit, I sat on the balcony and finished my blunt. I didn't want to argue with her, so I hopped on a cloud.

When I went back into the room, Purple had changed into her night clothes and got in the bed. Seeing as though she had a little attitude, I was prepared to adjust it with some good dick. However, she denied my advances. She said that I was cut off until I was a single man. Honestly, I wasn't threatened by it because I knew that Purple wasn't strong enough to deny me for long. She was always on me; therefore, it wouldn't be long before she'd be jumping on a nigga again. So, I didn't worry about it, I just did what I did best worked.

Now that our new stash spot was secured and the young dudes were handling the drop-offs and pick-ups, I could focus on sniffing out the snitch. Of course, my first stop was Helaina's. She was my most reliable source and I didn't have time to waste.

"I knew I'd see you again." Helania chuckled, opening her door. "What happened to never coming back?"

Shaking my head, I responded, "Man, it's a crazy story. Can we chop it up?"

She stepped back to let me enter then I followed behind her to the living room. Helaina was 44 and she was bad as a muthafucka. She had a perfect shape and the prettiest face ever. She could easily pass for 30 on her worst day; that was how bad she was.

"You want something to drink?" she asked, taking her seat.

"Nah, I'm good."

"So, what brings you back to Texas?"

"I'm 'bout to be a dad."

"Whaat? Congratulations. Who's the mother?"

"Purple."

Helaina's facial expression instantly turned into a look of shock. She knew all about my relationship to Em-kay and Purple. However, she knew nothing about the falling out.

"Em-kay shot you, didn't he?" she inquired. "'Cause you was fuckin' Purple. That's why you wouldn't tell me what happened that night. I knew it was something because it ain't like you to run from nothing. So, how are things?"

"We came to an agreement and worked it out. We good. That ain't why I came by, though. I need some information."

"Of course, you do. And I'm sure I know what info you need, but humor me."

"A few weeks back, the DEA raided our warehouse. Em heard them say they had an informant. I need to know who that is."

Helaina had a half smoked blunt in the ashtray that she fired up. She sat back and took a few puffs before looking back at me.

"You know, almost a year ago, my dad sat right there and asked me the same thing. He told me that the DEA had raided his warehouse and he heard something about a CI. It just so happened that his warehouse was robbed right before the bust, so they didn't find anything."

Listening to her talk had all type of shit going through my head. It wasn't a coincidence that the same shit that happened to Homer happened to us. My first thought was that the police we had on payroll moved the keys. However, they didn't get wind of the bust until it was happening. The only other person I could think of was the plug, Estelle. She was the common denominator but that didn't make sense because she wanted Em-kay to bring her the thief. She could be fucking with his head, though. For sure, my head was fucked with.

"Sas, listen to me," Helaina said, bringing me back out my thoughts. "I'ma tell you just like I told my daddy. Garrett is the CI. My daddy didn't want to believe that his best friend of fifty years would turn on him. But I've seen Garrett more than a few times at the county, looking like he wasn't trying to be seen. I can't prove it, but I know Garrett sent them guys to rob the gambling shack that night. I know he did."

"I believe you, Laina. I never trusted that fat bastard from the start. It's alright, 'cause he gon' get his."

"Sas, you can't just kill informants. If he dies, they will come for y'all."

"Even if he just disappears?"

"If they really want you locked up, they'll just find another CI. All I can tell you is to be careful. Don't give them a reason to mess with you. After a few months with nothing, they'll be forced to close the investigation."

I wasn't about to risk that shit, but I nodded anyway. Before I did anything, I was going to verify that Garrett was indeed the informant first. One mistake could send our entire crew to prison. I had to be sure about everything and plan the perfect murder.

"Did Homer ever find out who took his stash?"

"Nah. The crazy thing about it, was that they put it back a few days later."

I couldn't wait to tell Em about that shit. My mind went back to my second thought, *maybe Estelle got somebody to move the shit.* That

was the only thing that made sense at that moment. It was her product, and I was sure that she would do anything to protect it and
herself. If Em was caught with drugs, the DEA would want to know
who his plug was. I needed to talk to my bro asap because it was a lot
of strange shit going on.

Already knowing that Em-kay was out to lunch with Purple, I
headed over to the 'jects to visit Trina. That morning, I had my lawyer
file a petition with the courts for a divorce, so I wanted to let her
know before she got the papers. Just as I pulled up on the block, my
cell rang through the car's Bluetooth. It was the lawyer that I had
hired for my mama's case, so I answered quickly.

"Hello?"

"Hey, Mr. Aujour, how are you?"

"I'm good. What's up?"

"Well, the case was approved for a hearing. We'll go up in front of
the judge tomorrow and see if we can get the conviction overturned
or a retrial for lesser time."

"Do I need to be there?"

"No. It's a closed court. I'll call you soon as it's over."

"A'ight."

I hung up with the lawyer then hopped out my ride. Even with it
being cold out, the block was jumping as always. Before going up to
Trina's, I shot the shit with a few cats outside. Everybody was
showing mad love since I had been gone so long. Though my Haitian
family was welcoming, Dallas felt more like home. It had raised me,
so I was a little biased. Yet and still, Dallas was where I felt most
comfortable.

When Trina opened her door, she just stood there looking me
over. I could tell that she was surprised to see me, but I also saw that
she wasn't too happy.

"What's going down?" I asked, breaking the silence.

"Why I gotta hear from the streets that you back in the 'hood?"

"You gon' invite me in or what?"

She stepped back to let me enter. I eyed her as I strolled past her
then went back to her bedroom. Not only was my visit to inform her

about the divorce, I had to get my stash from there. With Purple trip-ping, I needed that to be my last visit to Trina's. I didn't want to have to choke her ass over nothing.

"Where you been, Sas?"

"You questionin' me like you my girl or somethin'."

"Technically, I am yo' wife, so I have every right."

"Yeah, about that," I said, throwing the last stack of cash in my backpack then turning toward her. "I filed for divorce this morning. You'll be gettin' the papers soon."

"Who is she? You want a divorce from me, so you must plan on marryin' somebody. So, who is she?"

"Trina, I'on owe you no damn explanation. I just wanted to give you a heads up about the papers. That's it."

I started toward the living room and Trina was right on my heels talking smack. Unlike Purple, Trina's mouth didn't bother me, so I let her run it.

"You owe me something. I held you down all these years. Hell, if it wasn't for me, yo' ass wouldn't even be a citizen. I ain't never ask yo' ass for nothin' in return. Not even respect. The least you could do is tell me why you disappeared for months then show up askin' for a divorce."

"I went to Haiti to handle some business, a'ight?"

"Is that why Em-kay showed up at my door months ago lookin' for you? 'Cause from the look of it, you were runnin' from him. What's goin' on?"

"Ain't nothin' goin' on. Nothin' that concerns you, anyway."

Trina's lips grew tight as she folded her arms across her chest. I hadn't fucked with Trina strong in a minute, so a nigga didn't have no feelings about how she felt. Purple was the only person I ever explained shit to, and that was only because of the situation. Well, and the fact that she had knocked my ass in the mouth. I couldn't play her like I could them other bitches.

"Well," Trina started, "if you want me to sign those papers, you need to pay me."

I chuckled. "What?"

"You heard me right. All the shit I did for you, and you just gon' ask for a divorce and leave with no explanation? You owe me. Years ago, you told me you would get me out the 'hood. I'm still here. So, if you want me to sign those papers, I need money to get out of here."

I couldn't even argue with her on that because I did promise to get her out the 'hood. But I was young then, and she was putting that pussy on me. Once I got a taste of more good pussy and better head from another bitch, those words faded in the wind.

"A'ight, I got you," I stated then walked out.

Honestly, I didn't know if I was going to even give Trina that money or not. I just needed to dead that conversation before it turned ugly. The nerve of that bitch trying to extort me out some money. That was alright, though, I'd handle that shit later. On my way back to my ride, I removed my burner phone to call Em-kay. His little lunch date with Purple should be over.

"What's goin' down, bro?" he answered.

"We need to talk."

"A'ight. I gotta take Bree to her doctor's appointment. Meet me at the crib 'bout eight."

"I'll just fall through in the morning. I been gone all day, so I'ma spend some time with Purple. She kinda mad at me."

"Yeah, she told me about Trina."

My marriage to Trina was something that I wanted to keep under wraps. I didn't want anyone knowing about it. Purple was in her feelings, so I should have known that she was going to say something to Em about it. Now I was going to have to explain to my bro why I didn't tell him.

"But we ain't gotta talk about that right now. I'll see you tomorrow."

"A'ight. Bet."

Pulling up to the house, I saw Peanut and Me Me loading his truck up. It was about time they came over and got all that shit out the way. I'd put it in the room downstairs that I had decided to turn into a mancave. Purple took it upon herself to redecorate my house, so I needed a space for myself.

"Bro, what's up?"

"Ain't shit," I replied, dapping Peanut up. "'Bout time y'all came and got this shit."

"Man, I ain't even know she had all this shit over here. Where you been?"

"Workin'. I got intel on who the snitch is." Peanut and I eyed each other for a moment. "Garrett."

"You said it was that nigga. What we gon' do?"

"I got to talk to that nigga Em first. I'm gon' talk to him in the morning about it. Meet me over there 'bout 8."

"Bet."

After helping Peanut and Me Me load the rest of the gifts in his SUV, they left. Purple was nowhere around, so I traveled up the stairs and found her stretched out across the bed. I swore, she was like a baby so cute when they're sleep, but hell on wheels while awake. I placed my hand on her stomach as I leaned over to kiss her forehead. Instantly, her eyes popped open.

"It's just like a nigga to eat then go to sleep," I joked.

She giggled, sitting up. "What else you 'pose to do after you eat?"

Purple pulled herself up to her knees then leaned in to give me a real kiss. Although a nigga was skeptical about her friendliness, I didn't make nothing out of it. Now, if she would have cooked me dinner, then I would've been apprehensive.

"I see ya gettin' ya lil' weight up," I toyed, squeezing that ass. "You almost fine again."

"Boy, fuck you." She laughed, pushing me away. "I'm fine now."

"Almost. Now me...I'm the definition of fine."

"Mm," she moaned before kissing me and rubbing her hand over my chest. "I ain't gon' front, you are fine as fuck."

"Fine enough to get a lil' bit of pussy? I just want a lil' bit."

She released a half smile. "I'm not doing it for you, I'm doing it for me. We ain't had sex that many times, and that dry spell got me horny."

I didn't give a fuck about why she was giving me some, I just needed to know that I could get it. Everything else was irrelevant to me. She gave in just like I knew she would, and I was going to take advantage of that. I was going to fuck her so good, that she would never even think about trying to hold out on me again.

22

EM-KAY

Bree had been on my ass about putting all the baby stuff she'd ordered together. Every day for the past two weeks, the delivery man was ringing the doorbell. If I didn't know any better, I would've thought something was going on between the two. I was tired of hearing Bree's mouth about it, so when my boys dropped by, I made them help me while we conversed.

"That ain't even how that shit go," Peanut barked. "Are y'all niggas reading the instructions or just lookin' at the box?"

"Nigga, this *is* how it go," Sas spat back. "See, it fits."

"It ain't a damn guessin' game. You gotta put the shit where it go, unless you want that lil' nigga to hit the floor. Trust me, I don' put this shit together before."

I picked up the instructions to look at them.

"He'll be a'ight," Sas continued. "All babies hit the floor at some point."

Peanut chuckled. "Crazy as you and Purple are, y'all kid *deflee* don't need to hit the floor."

"Don't talk about my son, man."

"Nigga shut up. His nut sack ain't even dropped yet and you already emotional."

"Peanut's right," I interjected. "That piece don't go right there."

"Well, I already screwed it in, so that shit going right there."

"How many men does it take to put a bouncer together?" Bree laughed, stepping into the nursery. "Obviously, more than three."

"It'll probably take the whole crew," Purple toyed. "Whateva you do, don't let them put my nephew crib together."

"A-ke-ke," Sas mocked them. "Make yaself useful and fix a nigga some breakfast or something."

"Ain't," she stated then strutted away.

Bree and Me Me laughed then strolled off behind her.

"I swear, I wanna punch her ass to Pluto sometimes," Sas groaned.

"Punch me to Pluto!" Purple yelled back from a distance. "And I'ma knock yo' ass to Neptune!"

We all started laughing; you could hear the girls laughing in the distance. Sas chuckled to himself while shaking his head. I shook mine, too, because I knew that he had hell on his hands. Her entire life, we had taught her to be strong and not to take no shit. She caught on quickly; too bad Sas was the one that had to deal with it. Then too, he helped groom her, so he knew what to expect.

Finally, we got the bouncer together and started on the crib. We had talked the entire time, yet Sas hadn't brought up the snitch. That was the main reason for their visit. I was impatient; therefore, I brought it up.

"Yo', but what's the 411, though?"

"It's exactly who I said it was." Sas eyed me. "Garrett's bitch ass."

It wasn't a total surprise that it was Garrett. The nigga did seem salty about the fact that Homer gave me the plug instead of him. However, I thought the nigga was cool about it. He hadn't complained since that day and he hadn't tried to get over since Sas checked his ass.

"You sure, my nigga? Without a doubt?"

"My source is pretty reliable. I'm gon' put them youngins up on him, though. Let them watch him for a few days."

"OK. What about that other thing? Mouse ain't found nothing yet?"

"From what he told me," Peanut spoke, "this muhfucka is professional. They avoided every camera around the warehouse, except one, and the view isn't good. All he could tell me, was that it was one person that did it."

That wasn't telling me shit. I didn't know one person in the city that could pull off a job like that. We hadn't stepped on any toes to cause someone to want to fuck with us, so I didn't know the reasoning behind the dope being taken and put back. What I did know, was that someone was showing us that they could get to us if they wanted to.

"My source told me that the same thing happened to Homer," Sas mentioned. "They said his stash got hit, the DEA raided it then the stash was put back. I'm thinkin' it's that Estelle bitch. She's the plug, so she knows where her distributors keep they shit. She's only at risk if her distro is at risk. Why not protect y'all?"

Sas was right, but I still didn't think that Estelle took the time out to move the drugs herself. She would be putting herself at risk if she did that. If she knew about the raid, I was sure that she would have contacted me to move the drugs. However, I couldn't rule her out. She could be fucking with my head to see how I handled business. Either way, I wasn't too worried about it. Like I said before, if she cut me off, it was fine with me.

By the time we got the crib together, the smell of food caught our attention. We made our way downstairs to the kitchen, where Me Me was whipping up breakfast. Bree was scrolling on her phone probably ordering some more shit—and Purple was standing next to the stove, stealing bacon.

"Look at 'em. Stampedin' in here," Purple joked.

"Look at you," I responded. "Eatin' up all the bacon."

"Mind yo' business. Me Me said I can have this."

Peanut strolled up behind Me Me and hugged her from the back.

"Ugh, y'all look so ugly together." Purple laughed.

"You a hater," Me Me shot back.

"So."

I couldn't help but laugh. She and Sas killed me with that. 'So' was their response to everything. That shit was crazy. Maybe they were meant for each other. Shit was still weird to me, but I had accepted them. And the fact that Purple was having a kid of her own, my little sister had grown up on me and I had to let her blossom.

The dining room was silent as we all chowed down on the breakfast Me Me had prepared. I had never witnessed such silence from the usual rowdy bunch. As I looked around the table, I smiled internally. Our team was solid, and we had some solid females backing us. The funny thing was, the exact women we promised not to deal with, were the same women that held us down. Life was full of twists and turns which was the main reason why rules shouldn't be made off emotions.

"Damn, Me Me," Sas smacked. "Yo' ass can throw down."

"Hell yeah," Peanut added. "My girl is the shit in the kitchen."

They were spitting straight facts because it was some of the best food I'd had in a minute. I mean, I did good in the kitchen, but it had nothing on Me Me.

"So, what you waitin' on, Nut?" I questioned.

"On her." Peanut eyed Me Me as he stuffed a forkful of food in his mouth. "To stop playin' and let me have all of her."

"Ain't nobody playin'," Me Me shot back. "Nobody but yo' bald-headed ass baby mama."

"She still givin' you hell?" I inquired.

"She tryin', but I just been ignorin' her ass."

"Finally," Sas added. "I been told you to ignore her ass, anyway."

"Why you ain't ask Sas what he waitin' on?" Purple toyed, winking at me.

"Here we go," Sas said, exhaling hard.

"Where the fuck we goin'?"

"Man, don't act like I ain't ask."

"You ain't ask me nothing, you suggested it. And you didn't even have no ring."

"A'ight." Sas stood up. "I'ma head out."

We all laughed at him. I stood up and followed behind him. Ever since Purple told me about him being married to Trina, I'd been wanting to talk to him about it. I was aware that she was one of the first bitches he banged, but married? The reason he gave Purple made sense; I was just wondering why he never mentioned it before.

"You good, my nigga?" I spoke as I pulled a blunt from behind my ear and sparked it up.

"I'm straight. You know yo' sister like to get under muhfucka's skin."

"You know I know. What's up with the situation with Trina, though? Why you ain't tell me about that shit?"

"'Cause it wasn't shit. I just needed ID and shit. I already filed for the divorce." I passed him the blunt, so he paused to take a few puffs. "That bitch want me to pay her to sign the papers."

"And what you gon' do?"

"I really wanna snap that hoe's neck." He took a long drag then passed the blunt back. "But I'm tryna do shit different. Remember when you told me that if I had something to live for I would calm down? Well, all I can think about is meetin' my son. I don't wanna do nothing that'll 'cause me not to be there for him. So, I'ma throw her some cash and be done with it."

"How much she askin' for?"

"No amount. Just enough to get out the 'hood."

"Let me handle it," I suggested, and Sas eyed me. "Nah, I'ma handle shit right."

One of the things I knew about females, was when their feelings got hurt, they would do whatever to get back at a nigga. It was nothing keeping her from asking for more shit after Sas paid her. I wasn't going to play with her, and I wasn't going to pay her shit.

"A'ight, but what I need help with, is gettin' Purp a ring. I gotta do everything I can to shut her the fuck up. Her ass ain't let up since I came back to this bitch."

"And she ain't until she get what she want. She spoiled. My bad, my nigga," I joked. "I'm glad she off my ass. The best advice I can give you, is to feed her ass every hour, hour and a half."

"I got you, bro."

Just as we finished that conversation, the front door opened. Purple sashayed out the door toward us. Though Sas was quiet, you could see the 'aww, shit' look he was rocking. On God, I wanted to laugh hard as fuck. She was giving my nigga the blues. I had never seen Sas timid before.

"You mad at me?" Purple smiled, securing her arms around Sas. "You know I just be messin' with you."

"Yo' ass need to stop. I don' told you."

"Why? Shit would be boring if I didn't act up."

"You get on my fuckin' nerves, you know that?"

"I'll *get* on something alright." She giggled then Sas leaned down to kiss her.

My first thought was to say something smart. However, I decided to let them have their moment. Besides, Sas looked as if he needed a break. I knew that look all too well. His ass was in love and fighting the urge to knock Purple's head off. To see him show so much restraint, led me to believe that he was changing. The fact that he'd rather pay Trina than to just off her, proved it. The old Sas would have dropped her where she stood. I was proud of my bro. He was becoming the man that I knew was inside of him. And surprisingly, I found myself completely happy for them.

23

BREELYNN

It was the day of the Christmas party and I was still getting everything together. After picking up the items I needed, I drove over to the 'ject. Rocco stayed two nights with us then decided that he'd rather be in the 'hood. I fought it tooth and nail because he was too young to stay by himself. However, Em-kay thought that we should give him a chance to prove himself. I didn't like the arrangement, but there was nothing I could do about it.

When I pulled up to the 'jects, the first person I saw was Chelle. She was standing on the sidewalk arguing with Puma. Instead of going over to speak, I waved then proceeded to my mama's apartment. As I approached the door, I could hear my mama fussing. My first thought was to turn and leave. I hadn't seen my mama since she tried to jump on me months ago. And still, I wasn't ready to see her, but that wasn't going to stop me from checking on my brother.

Instead of using my key to enter the apartment, I knocked on the door. Quickly, the door opened, and my mama was standing there scowling at me.

"Look what the fuck the wind blew in," my mama stated, blowing her cigarette smoke toward me. "What the fuck yo' fat ass want?"

"I came to check on my brother. Where is Rocco?"

"Don't worry about my child. I got him."

"Obviously not, because he been at Grandmother's house. And she's been lookin' for you."

"I don't give a damn, get the fuck off my porch!"

"Where's Roc?"

"Bitch, get the fuck away from my doe!"

She slammed the door on me. I was just about to turn and leave when the door swung back open. Rocco stepped out and closed the door behind him.

"Yo, Bree, what's up?"

"I came to check on you. You good?"

"Yeah, I'm good...Bree, Mama on drugs."

"What you talkin' 'bout?" I asked, acting clueless.

"I just caught her. I came in the house to get something to drink and she was in here sniffing coke. The coke Em gave me to sell."

Hearing that Em-kay gave Rocco drugs to sell, pissed me off instantly. True enough, Rocco told me out his own mouth that he wanted to hustle. He told me that he wanted to be like Em-kay. I couldn't be a hypocrite and tell him that it was the worst career choice while supporting Em-kay. Still, I didn't want my brother taking risks. Just as that thought crossed my mind, Rocco's friend, Eric, strolled up and dapped him up.

"Hey, Bree," Eric spoke.

"Hey, Eric. Rocco "

"Bree, I already know what you gon' say. Please don't start, Em got me. I'm good."

There was nothing more I could say to Rocco to change his mind, so I decided to leave it alone. It wasn't going to do nothing but stress me out, anyway. So, I started back toward my ride. Chelle was still standing out on the sidewalk looking pissed.

"What's going on, Chelle? You good?"

"Girl, Puma's bitch ass tryna play me for a damn fool. His phone was dead all night, and he tryna act like he was sleep the whole time. He don't even know that I caught a ride to his house last night and he wasn't there."

"You think he cheatin'?"

"I know he talkin' to some other bitch. When we were together yesterday, I saw him textin' another bitch, out the corner of my eye. That was the main reason I blew him up and went by last night. I ain't even worried about it, though. Fuck that broke ass nigga. What you doing over here?"

"Came to check on Rocco while I was out pickin' up some last minute stuff for the party."

"Good. Since you're here, I'ma catch a ride with you, so I won't have to look for one later."

"That's cool. That way you can help me setup. Where Sasha?"

"I ain't seen her since yesterday."

"Oh. Well, hurry up and go get yo' shit, I gotta get back home before Em-kay."

OF COURSE, Em-kay beat me home, and he had been talking shit ever since. No lie, the sound of his voice was aggravating me. Now I completely understood how he felt when I used to go on and on about stuff. I mean, it had been hours and he was still going.

"OK, Em, damn! You been sayin' the same shit for hours. I get it. You mad. But ain't shit happen."

"What if it did?"

"It didn't! And if it did, I'm far enough along that he'll be alright. Bae," I said, placing my hands on his face and pulling him in for a kiss. "Everything is alright. Stop stressing."

"A'ight," he replied then kissed me again. "But I know one thing, I ain't wearin' that ug-lass sweater you got me."

I laughed. "Yes, you are."

"Nope, not gon' do it."

"Whateva. Wit'cho boring ass."

The doorbell rang, so I went to answer it while Em-kay's slow ass finished getting dressed. If he wasn't on my ass so hard, he would have been dressed. By the time I made it to the stairs, Chelle was already opening the door. Peanut and Me Me strolled in looking festive. She even got him to wear an ugly Christmas sweater.

"It's cute in here," Me Me sang.

"Thanks, boo."

"I helped." Chelle laughed, hugging Me Me.

While we hugged and chatted, Peanut went directly to the kitchen. A few minutes later, Em-kay came down and joined him. We were just about to join them, when the doorbell rang again. It was Monty, and right behind him were Juke and his girl, Chyna. Just as I was about to close the door, Purple and Sas walked up. After greeting each other, we all traveled to the kitchen.

The Christmas music was playing, drinks were flowing, and everybody was having a good time. As I suspected, the guys were huddled together conversing while us females did the same. That was exactly what I didn't want. Noticing that Chelle and Monty were there alone, I decided to play matchmaker.

"Chelle, what you think about Monty?"

"He a'ight," she replied, looking over at him.

"You're here alone, he's here alone..."

"Wait, what happened to Puma?" Me Me questioned.

"Yeah." Purple added.

"Fuck Puma," I stated. "She need a nigga like Monty. Our girl deserves to be spoiled."

Chelle chuckled. "I can't argue with that."

"Good. Now let me go work my magic."

Before I could get over to Monty, the doorbell rang once again. That time, it was Sasha at the door. Of course, she came in extra loud.

"Merry Christmas," she cheered then rubbed my stomach. "Oh my god, Bree. Look at you."

"I know, right?" I chuckled, pulling her in for a hug. "Hey, girl."

After our embrace, we joined everybody in the living room. I noticed that Chelle hadn't maneuvered toward Monty yet. Smiling at her, I started toward Monty. Chelle had the look of embarrassment on her face as she turned and headed to the kitchen.

"Hey, Monty," I spoke, approaching him. "Come here, let me ask you something."

All the guys were staring hard at me. I winked at Em-kay while pulling Monty to the side.

"What's up, Bree?"

"What you think about my girl, Chelle?"

Monty pressed his eyebrows together. "What you mean what I think?"

"I mean, she's single, she's cute...You single?"

"Something like that. What's up with her, though? Why she ain't come ask me?"

I grabbed Monty by his arm and drug him into the kitchen where Chelle was. She was trying her best to look busy, but I saw her ass when she turned her back to us. Just when I was about to formally introduce the two, Sasha brought her ratchet ass in the kitchen.

"Hey, Monty," Sasha sang.

"What's up?"

"Chelle," I interjected. "Monty gon' help you get the gift bags out the garage."

"I'll help," Sasha volunteered as the doorbell rang again.

"Nah, I got something else I want you to help me with."

I grabbed Sasha's hand and pulled her out the kitchen behind me. Em-kay was opening the front door as we passed the foyer. Immediately, Sasha snatched her hand away from me and placed it on her hip.

"Oh, yeah?" Sasha stated.

Em-kay and I instantly looked at each other. Confusion was on both of our faces. I wasn't exactly sure why Em-kay was confused, but I had several questions. Reef was standing in the foyer with his arm around Me Me's sister Erin's neck. As confusing as that was, I still was wondering what Sasha was referring to.

"Man, gone on with all that," Reef stated.

"Wait," Erin said, confused. "What the fuck is going on, Reef?"

"Ain't shit going on."

"Oh, so me suckin' you and fuckin' you ain't shit?"

Soon as those words left Sasha's mouth, Erin punched her in it. Then, she turned and knocked the shit out of Reef. By that time, Sasha was coming with her right hook and hit Erin in her ear. Out of nowhere, Me Me ran up and snatched Sasha to the ground.

"Bitch don't hit my sister, hoe! She pregnant!"

"Really, bitch!" Sasha screamed, peeling herself up from the ground. "Yo' sister hit me! You know I'on have no problem fightin' a pregnant bitch if she wanna rumble."

"Not my sister, you ain't."

Sasha tried to lunge at Erin again, but Reef pushed her back.

"Touch her again bitch, and I'm gon' push yo' shit back," Reef threatened. "I ain't touched yo' ass in months. Get the fuck on with that dumb shit."

"What the hell going on?" Chelle asked from behind us.

Her question fell upon deaf ears because we were all waiting to see what was going to happen next. Sasha looked as if she wanted to swing again. Me Me looked like she was waiting on Sasha to swing. Purple was smiling hard as fuck while she stuffed her face. Chelle looked confused and Monty looked as if he knew exactly what was going on.

"Take me the fuck home, Reef," Erin stated then turned to go back out the door.

Of course, Reef ran out after her. That left Me Me and Sasha grilling the shit out each other. A few seconds went by then Peanut came and pulled Me Me toward the kitchen.

"Y'all some fake ass friends," Sasha complained.

"Girl, bye. Get the fuck on with that bullshit," Purple finally spoke. "Nobody even knew you was fuckin' with Reef. The fuck you thought, Me Me wasn't gon' have her sister's back?"

"Purple, shut the fuck up! You always got some smart shit to say."

Before Sasha completed her statement, Purple was up and on her way toward us. Sas hopped up, picked her up and carried her away before she could reach Sasha.

"Get the fuck out my shit!" Em-kay bellowed. "And don't bring yo' hoe ass around here no more!"

Honestly, I felt sorry for Sasha. She had gotten her feelings hurt, and people she considered friends turned against her in an instant. Yet and still, I was riding with Purple and Em-kay, for sure. There was no doubt about that. Plus, Sasha was always doing some hoe shit. So, I said nothing. Chelle grabbed her by the hand and they headed out the door. I felt so bad, but there was nothing I could do. It was what it was.

24

ME ME

The way my siblings embraced me when I pulled up to the 'ject almost made me feel bad. They were all over me as if I had done a 10-year bid. It had only been a few days since I had packed up and left, but you couldn't tell by the way they were clinging on to me. When I told them to go pack their overnight bag, they wasted no time going to do so. The entire time I waited at the door for them, my mama was looking at me like I had shit on my face. I was looking back at her the same exact way. I still couldn't believe that her ass was pregnant again.

"You ain't gon' be satisfied 'til you turn all my kids against me."

"I ain't tryna turn nobody against you. I'm just making sure they straight."

"The hell you ain't. Yana told me that you said she ain't got to listen to me."

I pursed my lips together and shrugged. I didn't tell Yana not to listen to her; that was her own doing. However, I wasn't going to make her mind someone that barely took care of her. Faye didn't deserve respect from her kids when she didn't even respect herself. Hell, I gave her more respect than she deserved. I wanted to tell her that and much more, but I decided to let her ass make it. It was Christmas Eve, so I wasn't about to let her fuck up my day. Instead of checking her ass, I headed toward the car.

"Me Me!" I heard Chelle call out.

"Hey, girl," I spoke when she got close to me. "What's up?"

"I was 'bout to ask you the same shit. What happened last night?"

I sighed. "Look, I ain't tryna beef with Sasha, but she knew I wasn't gon' let her fight my sister one on one. She knows better than anyone how me and my siblings get down. Her ass should've been beefin' with Reef, not my sister."

"I know, but damn, we all supposed to be friends."

"What you want me to do, Rochelle, apologize?"

"Being that you called me by my full name, I won't even ask. *But...* we all have been friends for too long, so I want y'all to work it out."

A horn blew, catching our attention. Monty had pulled up behind where I was parked and stepped out. I looked over at Chelle and she had the biggest grin on her face.

"Mm hmm," I hummed. "What's going on with y'all?"

"Nothing yet. He's taking me on a date, so we'll see."

"Call me and tell me everything."

We hugged then went our separate ways. My siblings were already piled up in the car waiting on me. They were super excited. I couldn't wait to see the looks on their faces Christmas morning, because I had gone all out.

We hardly ever ate out, so on our way to Peanut's, I stopped by Thibodeaux's to eat some seafood. When I pulled into the driveway at the house, my siblings began to 'ooh and ahh.'

"Damn, this shit phat," Dre boasted.

"Hell yeah," lil' Larry agreed.

"Me Me, this yo' house?" Precious inquired.

"This is Peanut's house. I'm just staying here."

"I wanna stay here," Darla mentioned as I killed the engine.

"Me too," Precious added.

"Well, you ain't," Yana snapped. "So, shut up and get out."

Obviously, Yana was still in her feelings about me moving out. A long talk with her was needed before I took them back home. The last thing I wanted, was for my sister to be bitter and taking it out on the younger ones. Peanut strolled out the front door with a smile on his face. Precious and Darla raced toward him. Dre and lil' Larry weren't far behind. I loved the fact that my siblings loved Peanut. And I could tell that he felt the same way. He always made sure to give them attention first.

Once inside, my siblings were running all over the place. I kept a close eye on them because I didn't want them to go out to the garage and see all the wrapped gifts. My plan was to wait until they were sleep before filling the tree. I put six empty boxes under the tree to fool them, and to keep the tree from looking empty. It was bad enough that I hadn't decorated it yet.

"They wired up." Peanut chuckled then kissed my forehead.

"I already knew they would be. What you been doing all day?"

"I did a lil' Christmas shoppin'." He smiled. "Oh, my mama gon' come spend the night with us."

"Did you talk to Ava about bringing Kairo?"

"Nah," he responded, rubbing his forehead. "I just let her be, man. I'm tired of all the back and forth. As much as I want to see my son, I ain't 'bout to let her hang that shit over my head. I'm done with that headache."

As good as that sounded, I couldn't let him give up on Kairo. He loved that little boy too much. Knowing that I was the reason that Ava wouldn't let him see Kairo gave me another thing to feel guilty about. The relationship I was in with Peanut brought me more joy than I could ever imagine. Still, it left me feeling guilty about a lot of things.

Finally, I got my siblings settled down by having them decorate the tree. Peanut and I sat, sipping eggnog that he made, laughing at my sibling argue over where to put each ornament. The doorbell rang, so Peanut got up to answer. He strolled back into the living room with his mama close behind. I had met Ms. Shunta months back when Peanut took me to Orlando with him. I guess real recognized real because we clicked right off. Truthfully, I think her hate for Ava made her like me even more.

"Hey, Me Me, girl," Ms. Shunta cheered.

"Hey, Ms. Shunta. How you been?"

"I've been good baby. Are these your sisters and brothers?"

"Yeah, that's them. Well, minus my big sister."

And the one my mama was carrying, I thought. While Ms. Shunta introduced herself to my siblings, Peanut's phone rang and he went upstairs to take it. I was curious about the call because Peanut never walked off to take a call before, but I didn't let it worry me. Instead, I continued with the activities I had planned. I took them to the kitchen so that they could make gingerbread houses. Precious and Kerry were too young to do it without help; therefore, I had them to help me make cookies from scratch.

"Stop eatin' up all the gum drops," Yana complained.

"Derriyana, shut up!" Darla exclaimed. "You not the boss of me."

"Somebody gotta be."

"Well. It ain't gon' be you."

"Y'all, chill out," I intervened. "Listen, I know a lot of things have changed, but that's what happens in life. We've dealt with change before and we were fine. Yana, I know you not happy about me movin' out, but don't take it out on everybody else. You know I love you, right? And I will always be there, right?"

"Yeah, I know."

Before speaking, I looked at each of them in their eyes.

"I love all y'all and we gon' be good. I know y'all probably look at this house and think it's the reason why I left, but it ain't. We ain't never had shit, so I'm used to that. Me and Mama not seein' eye to eye right now, and that's why I left."

"I understand," Dre spoke. "You grown now, Me Me, and you need a life. You was always at home with us."

"Yeah," lil' Larry added. "You been our mama for a long time. Me and Dre will hold down the fort."

I chuckled. "I appreciate it."

"Uh-oh," Ms. Shunta said, sashaying into the kitchen. "This where I need to be."

She washed her hands and joined right in. Though our conversation wasn't finished, I felt my siblings were understanding what I was telling them. I needed them to understand that the only thing that was changing, was my address. I would always be there for them. A few minutes later, Peanut entered the kitchen. He strolled over behind me then wrapped his arms around me.

"Let me talk to you real quick," he whispered in my ear.

I rinsed my hands then followed him to the living room. I was sure that we were going to talk about whatever his call was about. I just hoped that he didn't have to leave to work.

"What's going on?" I asked.

"She 'bout to bring Kairo."

"That's good, right?"

"Yeah, but I lied. I told her that you weren't here." I just stood there staring at him as he continued. "That was the only way I could get her to bring him."

"Whateva," I stated then turned to walk away, but Peanut pulled me back.

"Hey." He kissed my lips. "Don't be mad. I'm just playin' the game, so I can spend Christmas with my son."

"I said, whateva."

Soon as Peanut's lips parted, the doorbell rang. He kissed me once more before releasing me to answer the door. At first, I was going to go back to the kitchen with my siblings. However, the fact that Peanut had to lie to her pissed me off. I was so sick of that bitch holding Kairo over Peanut's head. He'd been acting cool about it, but I knew that it was fucking with him. He wasn't the same playful Peanut that I previously knew.

Peanut stepped outside the door and closed it behind him. So, I went over to the slim window that was next to the door to peek out. Ava was still holding Kairo while questioning Peanut. The whole time, Kairo was whining and reaching for Peanut.

"Why you won't let me come in? You must got that bitch in there."

"Ain't no bitch in there. If my bitch was in there, she woulda been out here on yo' ass by now. Now gimme my damn son."

"Why I can't come in then? Huh? I just wanna see how you decorated for Christmas. You claimed you had a tree and gifts for him. Let me see."

"You gon' give him to me or not?" Peanut spoke calmly. "'Cause what I ain't 'bout to do, is go back and forth with yo' ass. He sittin' here screamin' and you standin' here being a bitch."

"You being a bitch!"

"Daddy!" Kairo cried.

"Man, stop doin' 'em like that. Don't bring him over here just to make him fuckin' cry."

"Fuck you, nigga!"

"Gimme my fuckin' son, man!" Peanut growled as he stepped forward and grabbed Kairo from Ava. "I ain't 'bout to keep playin' wit'cho funky ass! Bitch, get off my porch, hoe!"

"I ain't goin' no muthafuckin' where!"

Now that Peanut had Kairo in his possession, I decided to show my face. *Fuck that bitch and the lie Peanut told her!* I pulled the door open then stepped out.

"What the fuck is the problem?"

"You the fuckin' problem, bitch!" Ava shot back.

"Why? 'Cause I fuck with the nigga you got a baby by? Hoe, bye. I'ma have a baby by his ass, too. Then what you gon' do, huh? I don' beat yo' ass twice, so you can't whoop me. Yo' baby daddy suckin' toes and bussin' nuts in me every night, so you ain't gettin' him back. I threw the rest of yo' shit away and put mine there, so you ain't movin' back in. It's over. Grow the fuck up and put yo' son first."

"Don't talk about my fuckin' son!"

Here we go. Every time you call a bitch out about her being a fucked up person, they want to get mad and claim you talking about their kids. *No, bitch, I'm talkin' about yo' triflin' ass!*

"You don't have kids, so don't tell me what to do with mine!" she continued. "I take damn good care of mine! You can't tell me shit!"

"Sooo," I sang. "Why you make him cry five minutes for his daddy? Yeah, thought so."

On that note, I grabbed Kairo from Peanut then went into the house. I wasn't in the mood to read her like a textbook. Folks swear, just because you don't have children, you somehow don't know the different between right and wrong. Or you somehow don't have common sense. Having a child of your own doesn't automatically qualify you to be a good parent. If that was the case, it wouldn't be so many fucked up individuals in the world. If that was the case, my mama would have raised her own kids. Shit, I had been raising kids before she even had one. *That bitch ran me hot!*

25

PEANUT

Once Me Me talked her shit, took Kairo and went back in the house, Ava was stuck. It took her a minute before she even looked back at me. I stood there staring her down, waiting on some fly shit to come out her mouth. Surprisingly, she didn't say shit. She looked at me briefly before turning and strutting away. I stood on the porch until her brake lights disappeared up the street.

By the time I got back inside, Me Me had sent all the kids upstairs to get ready for bed. She was bent over, removing the cookies from the oven. I strolled over behind her and secured my arms around her.

"I love you," I whispered in her ear.

"Mm hmm."

"I do."

"Obviously, I love you, too. I keep puttin' up with the bullshit."

"I'ono," I said, stepping from behind her. "She left here on mute, so she might chill out."

"I doubt it, but whateva. Get that gift bag off the island and open it."

"Aw, shit." I smiled. "I'm gettin' a early Christmas gift?"

"Don't think yo' walnut head ass is special. Everybody got one."

"The fuck is this?" I asked, pulling some green and white striped shit out the bag.

"Pajamas, put 'em on."

"Hell nah." I laughed. "I ain't 'bout to walk around here lookin' like a damn spearmint peppermint."

"Yes, the fuck you are. And I'm gon' take yo' picture, too."

"This shit is not gangsta. We gon' have to talk about this."

"You want some pussy tonight?"

"Hell yeah."

"OK. Talked about it. Go change."

"Hell nah," I groaned, strolling back toward her. "If I'm gon' even entertain the idea of puttin' that shit on, I gotsta get the pussy first."

"Uh-uh, move." She laughed, stepping backward. "We got a house full of people."

Without saying another word, I grabbed her hand and pulled her into the laundry room. I tongued her down while removing her jeans. Once I had them off, swiftly, I picked her up and placed her on the washer. Before I dug into her, I turned the washer on to drown out any noise we were about to make.

"Mmmm," Me Me released an extended moan when I entered her. "Shit, bae."

"Damn, you feel so good."

"You, too."

"I'm 'bout to put a baby in you. I can feel it."

"I just want you to fuck me good. Fuck that baby."

"I'm gon' do both."

Me Me secured her arms around me tightly then I fucked the shit out of her. Usually, I liked to take my time with her, but time wasn't on our side. I wasn't going to sweat it, though. Once the kids were sleep, I was going dig deep in them guts for a long time.

"That damn machine ain't covered up nothing," my mama chastised soon as we stepped out the laundry room. "Luckily I came down here before the kids."

"I'm sorry, Ms. Shunta," Me Me apologized.

"Don't be sorry, you grown. Be careful. Peanut..."

"Mama, don't even."

"Whateva, boy."

OUTSIDE OF ME Me making me wear the whack ass pajamas, I enjoyed my night. Mainly because I had my son back. The entire time we played games and watched movies, he never left my lap. My son missed me just as much as I missed him. It almost had me regretting shit. However, I was completely happy with Me Me. Though she had no problem with speaking her mind and running my pressure up, I loved the shit out of Me Me. She was smart, ambitious, she took care of home and me, and she never asked for nothing. She was the total package and that was why I wanted her to be mine forever.

It was 5:45 when Me Me woke me from a deep sleep. I was tired as fuck, so I didn't even want to open my eyes. Slowly, I cracked them open when Me Me kissed my lips.

"Merry Christmas." She giggled.

It looked like her ass had been up. She definitely had already brushed her teeth.

"Girl, lay yo' ass down," I groaned.

"Boy, get yo' ass up," she shot back. "It's Christmas."

Me Me's ass was more excited about Christmas than the kids. I think it was because they had no idea what was in store for them downstairs. Once everybody was sleep, I helped Me Me drag in all the shit that had been taking over my garage. It wasn't until I began to see my mama, Kairo and my name on several gifts, that I understood why there were so many. She literally bought a lot of gifts for everybody. That girl was so selfless, she deserved the world.

"I don't know why you excited. Santa didn't bring you shit."

"So." She laughed, pulling me up from the bed.

Once I was up, Me Me began to turn on all the lights and was yelling that it was Christmas. By the time I came out the room, the kids were rubbing their eyes as they slowly walked toward me. Me

Me stepped out of Kairo's room, holding him while he rubbed his eyes, too.

"Wooow!" Kerry sang, and everybody turned and looked at her.

Kerry had never spoken as far as I knew, so it stunned me to hear her speak. Obviously, it surprised everybody else because they were just looking at her. She started giggling and ran down the stairs. All the other kids began to yell and cheer as they ran down. Me Me had the biggest smile ever on her face.

"This one mine. This one mine," they began to fuss over the motor bikes that Me Me bought.

She got the boys mini motorcycles, the girls got mini four wheelers. Kerry, Precious and Kairo got power wheels.

"Calm down," Me Me called out as we walked down the stairs. "I'll tell y'all who gets what."

While she told them which was theirs, I grabbed Kairo and sat down with him. His eyes were wide open, but I could tell that he was sleepy as fuck. He just laid against my chest and watched everything. He finally got active when Me Me began to hand him gifts to open.

"See," Me Me said, taking a seat next to me. "This is all I wanted for Christmas. To see them smile. Look how happy they are."

I kissed her cheek. "Yeah, I get it."

"Look at Kairo." She giggled. "He just tearing paper."

I didn't even see my mama get up; next thing I knew, she was bringing us cups of hot chocolate. We sat there for a while watching them open all the shit Me Me had bought. From toys, to shoes, clothes, cell phones she had bought it all. I didn't know how she made that money stretch, but she had taken care of everybody.

The living room was a mess by the time the kids were through. Me Me had gotten them all duffel bags, so she had them to put their clothes there.

"Did y'all check the stockin'?" I asked, just as things died down.

They all looked back at the fireplace then took off running. I had placed jewelry boxes in each of them. The boys got chains while the girls got charm bracelets.

"Me Me, here yo' stockin'," Darla said, strolling toward us.

Me Me smiled at me as she took it from Darla. They all stood in place, looking to see what she got. She removed the top off the square box then squealed as she pulled the keys.

"I know you fuckin' lyin'. A Porsche, what?"

"Cayenne."

"Thank you, babe." She kissed me.

"You're welcome. Is that all you see in that stockin'?"

She stuck her hand in the stocking and felt around. Suddenly, she got completely still. While she stared at me, I released a smile. Slowly, she pulled her hand out and held the ring up.

"Alright, now," my mama sang.

"So, what's up?" I questioned, taking the ring from her. "You down or what?"

"Yes, baby. Of course, I'm down."

26

PURPLE

It had been months since I had kicked it in the 'hood. Now that I had put on a little weight, I was ready to see the world again. Mainly, I was just tired of being in the house. I had never been a homebody; therefore, I was over being cooped up. Especially since Sas had gotten me a new wardrobe for Christmas.

When I pulled up on the block, everybody and their mama was outside. Me Me's little brothers flew past me on the motor bikes she got them. Darriyana and Darla were padded up, flying right behind them. Me Me and Chelle were leaning on the hood of a bad ass Porsche Cayenne. I parked directly behind it and hopped out.

"Whaat?" Me Me sang. "Yo' ass out the house?"

"Girl, yeah." I chuckled. "I'm sicka that damn house. Hey, Chelle."

"Hey, baby mama," she spoke, rubbing my stomach.

"Who shit y'all chillin' on?"

"It was one of my Christmas gifts." Me Me smiled, holding her hand out.

"Biitch," I squealed. "I know you fuckin' lyin'."

Giggling, Me Me replied, "That was the same shit I said."

"You're definitely levelin' up," Chelle added. "Next thing you know, you gon' be rockin' a belly like Purple and Breelynn."

"What about you, though?" I inquired. "I saw you talkin' to Monty the other night. What's up with y'all?"

Chelle blushed hard. "We just friends right now. He cool, though."

I didn't know too much about Monty, other than the fact that he was part of my brother's crew. He was the quiet one out the bunch, which was perfect for Chelle. Chelle was one of the coolest females that I knew, and she was quiet until she needed to be.

"Y'all seen Sasha?" I asked.

Me Me immediately rolled her eyes.

"Yesterday," Chelle answered. "Y'all need to talk. Shit got way out of hand the other night.

"Did y'all know she was fuckin' with Reef?" I inquired.

"I didn't know nan one of 'em was fuckin' with him," Me Me responded. "Erin just told me she was pregnant, but I didn't know by who. Honestly, I don't care who they fuckin', I just wasn't 'bout to let her fight my sister."

Speaking of the devil, Sasha was strolling up the block in our direction.

"Here that hoe come," Me Me groaned.

"Me Me, chill," Chelle told her.

"Whateva."

I just stood there waiting for her to approach us because I knew she was. We were all the same. None of us were scary and we made it a point to let anyone we were beefing with know so. Sasha was the pettiest of us all; therefore, I knew she wouldn't let an opportunity to be that pass her by.

"Hey, fake ass hoes," Sasha murmured.

"Hey, single ass bitch," Me Me shot back.

"Not you, Chelle," Sasha continued without responding to Me Me. "What's up, girl?"

"Nothing much. Enjoyin' this lil' sun on a cool day."

"I feel ya. What got yo' tongue?" Sasha directed her question at me.

"I always got some smart ass shit to say, right? So, it's prolly best that I don't say shit to you."

My phone chimed, so I didn't bother to listen to her reply.

Baby: *Damn u lkn sxy frm da bck.*

Immediately turning around, I scanned the block for Sas. I didn't see him, but I knew that he was out there somewhere. He was always in the cut somewhere.

Me: *Come squeeze my booty.*

"You just gon' ignore me, huh?" I heard Sasha say.

"Girl, I'm flirtin' with my baby daddy. What the fuck you want?"

Baby: *Can I bend u ovr?*

Me: *Hell yeah.*

Just as I pressed send, I smelled Sas's cologne then felt him rub up behind me. He squeezed my ass a few times before securing his arms around my stomach. I leaned back and melted in his chest. It was our first time showing affection toward each other in public, so I was enjoying every second of it. Especially since Sasha looked jealous as fuck. I was just waiting on her to speak to Sas so I could check her ass. She knew better because she would hardly even look in his direction.

"I want you," Sas whispered in my ear. "Meet me at the house."

I giggled. "Bye, y'all."

"Where y'all going?" Me Me questioned.

"We'll see you tonight," Sas mentioned as he turned us around and walked me to my Jeep.

"What's tonight?" Me Me asked, but Sas didn't respond.

∼

"Purp," Sas called out. "Let's go."

Quickly, I rubbed my red lipstick over my lips then strolled out the bathroom. I didn't know why he was rushing me. It wasn't like we had a certain time to be at dinner. For the past hour, Sas had been rushing me to get ready. I'd kept my cool because I wanted us to have a full day without arguing, but he was pushing it.

"Why you rush "

I cut my question off because Sas was at the bottom of the stairs on one knee. Purple flower petals lined the staircase. Out of nowhere, tears began to stream down my face. I wasn't trying to be emotional, but I couldn't help it. Sas wasn't the type to do stuff like that; therefore, to see him put a little thought into proposing to me again, meant everything.

"You were right," Sas started. "I ain't even come at you right the first time. I got a ring this time, though. So, you gon' marry a nigga or what?"

Although tears were falling from my eyes, I giggled as I started down the stairs. I guess that was as good as it was going to get when it came to Sas's proposal. He was just too damn hood.

"I mean, I guess," I toyed. "Since you got a ring and shit."

"Cool."

Once I got to the bottom of the staircase and Sas slipped that fat ass rock on my finger, I forgot all about his ass being married to Trina. The only thing I could think about, was the fact that I finally had the man that I'd wanted for years. And now that the ring was on my finger, I was not letting him go. No matter what those papers said, T'Segai Aujour belonged to me.

27

SAS

Ever since I found out that Garrett was the snitch, I had been watching his every move. I had the youngins watching him when I wasn't. Just as Helaina said, Garrett was the snitch. I had personally watched him get in and out of an undercover's car twice. I knew it wouldn't be long before he tried to set us up, and that was exactly what he tried to do yesterday. He called Em-kay wanting to get 20 keys. Em already knew something was up because he never needed that many at the end of the month.

I told Em to set up the deal. Instead of meeting up with him, we had the youngins to watch his spot while we took the girls out. Right before we stepped in the restaurant, I got the call that undercovers were all over his place. Just as dessert was being brought to the table, Garrett was ringing Em's phone. Em gave him an excuse on why he didn't come through and rescheduled.

While Em-kay bullshitted Garrett, I already had a plan. Seeing as though undercover agents were always patrolling his spots, I knew that I couldn't taunt him, like I wanted to, before I killed his bitch ass. After dinner, I fucked Purple good and put her to sleep. I snuck out, heading to a location two blocks away from Garrett's house. It was a slim view from there to Garrett's bedroom. Once I put my sniper rifle together, I patiently waited.

The damn sun was coming over the horizon when Garrett finally started moving around his bedroom. Still, I waited patiently to make sure that no one was there with him. Once he stepped out the bathroom with the towel wrapped around his waist, I took my shot. It was right on the money. Afterward, I took a few seconds to scan the bedroom through the scope. There was no other movement, so I broke my gun down and jumped three buildings to make my exit.

Garrett being dead was going to shock the shit out of everybody. I didn't tell anyone that I was going to take Garrett out on purpose. Mainly because I knew the police would come asking questions. Their reaction to the news would be real versus them trying to fake it. Investigators could see right through that fake shit. I had my alibi together, so I wasn't tripping. I was at home sleep, and my phone location would prove it.

After getting rid of the gun, I went straight home. Quietly, I climbed the stairs then entered the bedroom. Purple was sitting up against the headboard, stuffing her face.

"Where in the fuck you been all night?"

"I had to handle something."

"That ain't gon' cut it. Tell me where the fuck you been or we 'bout to have huge problems."

I strolled over to the bed then sat next to her.

"I had to handle a snitch nigga, a'ight. Don't say shit to nobody. If the police ask, we fucked all night then went to sleep."

"If I find out anything different, I'ma handle *yo'* ass."

"Yeah, I know." I leaned over and kissed her stomach. "What's up, lil' man?"

Purple grabbed my hand and placed it where the baby was. My little man was moving around. I wouldn't lie, that shit felt weird. However, I was intrigued by it.

"Man, this shit wild." I smiled. "It's a whole baby in yo' stomach."

She giggled. "He ain't that big. Wait 'til I'm Bree size, you gon' see him moving from the outside. It's crazy."

"How many you wanna have?"

"However many you wanna have."

I pulled the cover off her then pulled Purple closer to me. I couldn't get enough of her ass. Even though Purple got on my nerves more than anyone, I loved her ass the most. Every time I was around her, I wanted to be all under her. She made me feel good. She made me feel like a man.

It wasn't long before I was tasting Purple's sweet nectar. I swore, I couldn't get enough of her ass. While I was away, I wasn't even thinking about her ass. Now, I was never not thinking about her. Never not thinking about us and our future. I wanted normality in my life, that was why I didn't entertain her trying to argue with me. We were about to be parents, so it was time out for all that drama.

"Oou, shit," Purple gasped when I eased into her.

"Damn, I can't get enough of yo' ass."

"You don't have to," she moaned. "It's yours forever."

"Damn right it is."

I tongued her down while stroking her slowly. Being inside of her was the best feeling ever. Her shit gripped me like no other. She had a nigga head over heels, deep in her love with her. Having her for the rest of my life wouldn't even be long enough to satisfy my appetite.

Purple and I got it in good before falling asleep in each other's arms. We were sleeping good as hell until someone began ringing the doorbell and knocking simultaneously. Being that we were both butt naked, we scrambled to find something to throw on. Before I left the room, I grabbed my gun then looked at Purple. She gave me a nod then I made my way down. I could see a car in the driveway, but it didn't look familiar to me.

Looking out the peephole, I saw that it was the lawyer that I had hired to handle my mama's case. I hadn't heard from him since they had pushed the hearing back, so I was surprised to see him at my door.

"What's up?" I answered, still standing in the doorway. "The fuck you ringin' my doorbell this early in the morning for?"

"T'Segai, watch your filthy mouth," my mama said, stepping from behind the post on the porch.

"Yoo," I sang as I reached over and hugged my mama. "Why y'all ain't call me?"

"I did. You were in the shower. I talked to your fiancée. Didn't she tell you?"

I looked back and Purple was standing on the stairs smiling. All I could do was shake my head before hugging my mama again. It had been so long since I had touched her. The last time I saw her, she was behind a glass window. Now that I had her in my arms, I didn't want to let her go. Finally, my life was coming together.

28

BREELYNN

It was New Year's Eve, and everybody agreed that we should go out to celebrate. Most of our gatherings had been at each other's houses, so we wanted to get out for a change. For once, Em-kay didn't even hassle me about it. We went to a few boutiques and found the perfect outfits. Soon as we got in the car to head home, I felt a little pain. It wasn't excruciating or nothing; therefore, I said nothing to Em-kay. I didn't want him using that as an excuse to keep me in the house that evening.

Just as we got in the car, my cell began to ring. My grandmother was calling, so I picked up quickly.

"Hey, Grandmother. What's going on?"

"Hey, baby. How are you feeling?"

"I feel good. I'm out and about."

"That's good to hear. I was calling because I finally caught up with Crystal. I stopped by her place and found her high out of her mind."

I didn't even know what to say to her. I knew sooner or later she was going to find out about my mama, yet and still, I didn't prepare myself for that conversation. Honestly, I was hoping that my grandmother didn't find out. She was too old to be dealing with the problems that we created for ourselves.

"What did she say?"

"She started talking shit about all of us, and about how grown she is, so I just got out of there. I ain't got nothing else to say to her until she gets her life together."

"Rocco didn't want to stay here with us, so I went by to check on him the other day. She cursed me out, too."

Em-kay shot me a look that I pretended not to see. I had forgotten all about him being in the car.

"Well, let 'em be. That's all we can do. How you been, baby?"

"I've been fine. Just left from shopping with Em-kay. We're going out tonight."

"Tell him I said, hi. Y'all be careful out there tonight."

"OK, Grandmother. I love you. I'll talk to you later."

Soon as I hung up the phone, Em-kay started questioning me about my mama cursing me out. I already knew that was coming. I didn't even argue with him, though. If I pissed Em-kay off, we would be going nowhere that night. So badly, I wanted to turn up with my girls one last time. Arguing with him wasn't worth the risk.

"Why you ain't tell me that Crystal cursed you out?" Em-kay questioned me again once we got home.

"'Cause it wasn't nothing."

"You know I don't like you going around there by yourself. What if she woulda started trippin' again?"

"Em, it was a week ago. Nothing happened. It's over and I ain't going back over there."

"Bree, I ain't tryna run you or tell you what to do, I just wanna keep you and my baby safe. Powder heads are unpredictable."

"I know, Em-kay. Can you drop it already?"

"A'ight," he groaned. "Whateva."

His phone rang and I was glad about it. I needed something to distract him to get him out my face. Since it always took me a while to get ready, I started early. I didn't need any other reason to hear Em-kay bitching about something.

A few hours later, Sas and Purple showed up at the house. While the guys began to pour up, Purple finished my hair and make-up for me. I was grateful, too, because my back was starting to hurt. Then, Me Me, Erin and Chelle showed up with Peanut, Reef and Monty. I was curious about how Reef and Erin hooked up, but I didn't bother asking. However, Purple did.

"Erin you been low-key," Purple spoke, side-eyeing her. "How you end up fuckin' with Reef?"

"Girl." She blushed. "Like always, Reef was on the block. I came out the corner store and he tried to holla. I made him walk me all the way back to the 'ject before I gave him my number. After that, we started fuckin' around. Y'all knew he was fuckin' with Sasha?"

"Nah," we all assured her.

"When we left here the other night, he told me that he used to pay her to suck his dick."

Knowing how Sasha was, Reef probably wasn't lying on her. She always had a little change, not much, and she had no job. Her mama was just as broke as the rest of our mamas, so she had to be getting money from somewhere.

"So, y'all official or what?" Me Me inquired.

"We're in the phase where he's beggin' and apologizin'. I'll forgive him tonight, though. Only 'cause he gon' be drunk and I know that dick gon' be good." She laughed.

"We all gon' be gettin' some good dick tonight," Purple added, still laughing.

"Yo!" I heard Em-kay yell. "The fuck y'all still doin' up there!"

"Shut up!" Purple yelled back, and we all laughed as we strolled out the bathroom.

As we traveled down the stairs, I suddenly felt as if I had to urinate. Then, I felt wetness between my legs. Immediately, I stopped because I just knew that I hadn't pissed myself.

"What?" Em-kay asked.

"I think I might've pissed on myself."

Everybody turned and looked at me. My clothes weren't wet, yet and still, I felt embarrassed. I turned to go back up the stairs and I felt the water running down my leg.

"You sure yo' water ain't broke?" Peanut stated.

By that time, Em-kay had slid his hand between my legs, feeling around. I didn't know what was going on, but I knew that my night out was cancelled. Em-kay's ass wasn't going to let me go nowhere.

"Come on, let's go to the hospital," Em-kay stated. "Y'all gon' ahead and go out. We going to get her checked out."

I wouldn't even lie; I was mad as hell. I was cute as fuck in my outfit and no one was going to get to see me in it. I marched back up the stairs and changed clothes before we headed to the hospital. I honestly hoped that I had the baby because I was over being pregnant.

29

EM-KAY

Seeing my son born, was an indescribable feeling. I never knew that the same thing that made my stomach turn, filled it with so much happiness. It instantly made me regret even more not letting the other ones make it. Though my little man came earlier than expected, the doctor said that he was okay. Still, we only got to hold him briefly before they took him to the NICU for labored breathing and jaundice.

"I'm proud of you, babe," I said, kissing Bree on the forehead. "You did real good."

"I'm so tired." She yawned. "How long they said it would be before they bring him back?"

"A few hours."

"He looks so much like you and Purp. That's crazy."

"That's them strong genes."

"I guess. You gon' go let everybody know he's here?"

"Yeah."

While I brought Bree to the hospital, everybody else went out. After they left the club, they all came up to the hospital. Bree was still in labor, so I told them that they didn't have to stay. Everyone left, but Sas and Purple came back a few hours later.

When I strolled into the waiting room, Purple was in Sas's lap sleep. His head was laid on top of hers and he was sleep, too. I stuck my finger in Purple's nose and she woke up talking shit.

"Get yo' stankin' ass fingers out my nose, nigga."

"My finger don't stink, punk."

"Smell like you dug in yo' ass." She laughed then stretched. "Is my nephew here yet?"

"Yeah, he's here."

She hopped up. "Let's go see him."

"Congrats, bro." Sas dapped me up.

We caught the elevator up to the NICU. While we rode up, I told them what was going on with him. Once we got to the nursery window, Purple immediately picked him out. It wasn't hard because he looked like our asses. They had him under a light with a little oxygen mask next to his face. He was laid up there with his legs cocked wide open like he had big nuts. He was definitely my seed.

"Aw, my nephew is so cute," Purple cooed. "I can't wait to hold him."

"Dude look just like you," Sas stated. "Damn, that's crazy."

"He got on her nerves enough," Purple retorted. "Of course, he was gon' come out lookin' like yo' ass. He's cuter than you, though."

I chuckled. "Whateva, big head ass girl."

We stood in the window for a while just starting at the new addition to our family. I couldn't wait to get him home and start our journey. After looking at the baby, we went back down to Bree's room.

Pushing the room door open, I was met by two men in suits. I frowned as I walked farther into the room because Agent Asshole was standing by Bree's bedside.

"Yo, what the fuck is going on?" I questioned.

"Em-kay Hart and T'Segai Aujour, just the two men I need to talk to."

"You don't need to talk to me about a muthafuckin' thing," I assured him. "I told you I'on sell no fuckin' drugs."

"We ain't here about drugs. Oh, no. This is about a homicide."

"One thing is for sure, I don't know what the fuck you talkin' 'bout. I ain't killed nobody. I don't even know who dead."

"I'm Detective Summers," one of the suited men spoke. "We want to talk to the both of you about the murder of Garrett Evans."

Again, I frowned. "What the fuck? Garrett got murked?"

"Don't try and act surprised," Agent Asshole continued. "Now, you can come down to the station voluntarily or I can get a warrant and search wherever I want for evidence."

I looked over at Sas and that nigga was as silent as a church mouse. Looking at him, I couldn't tell if he did the hit, pushed the button on it or knew anything of it. He just had a blank expression on his face.

"Look, man," I started, "my wife just had my baby, y'all got to wait."

"It's OK, baby," Bree spoke. "I already told them we was at home when he was killed. Go answer their questions and come right back."

"T'Segai was at home with me, too," Purple spoke.

"We just got a few questions," Detective Summers spoke. "We heard that you all work together, so we just need to clear up a few things."

Though I was not in the mood for their shit, I decided to go along with them. I had no idea of who killed Garrett, so I wasn't worried about getting booked. Sas, on the other hand, I didn't know what he knew. Since we were in the presence of detectives, there was no way that I could ask him about it. All I knew was that I wasn't under arrest and I wasn't staying at the station long. Soon as they started with the bullshit, my ass was out. I had a family to worry about. I didn't have time for any extra shit.

Once we got to the station, they placed Sas and I in different rooms. I already knew that was coming, though. I texted Bree to see if they had brought her our son, and they still hadn't. That was good news for the police because if they had, my ass would be out.

"OK, Mr. Hart," Detective Summer started, strolling into the room. Agent Asshole was with him.

"If this is a homicide investigation," I interrupted, "what the fuck he doing here?"

"Because he sold drugs for you," the asshole replied. "And because I know you had something to do with his death."

"Whateva, man. I ain't even know the nigga was dead. I been at the hospital all night, so how the fuck could I kill him?"

"He wasn't killed last night," the detective said. "He was killed two days ago."

"Two days ago, I was with my boys all day. That night, me and my boys took our girls on a date then we went home and fucked on them all night. We ain't did shit to that nigga."

The detective had me run down my timeline, hour by hour for that day. He asked me if I had any other proof that I was home all night and morning, and I did. I had cameras all over my house. Agent Asshole looked pissed about it, too. Yet again, I had beat him at the game he was playing solo. He was so hell bent on locking me up, that he was fucking up everything.

"Can I go now?"

"Give me one minute, Mr. Hart," Detective Summer said, standing to his feet. "I'll be right back then you can go."

He exited the room, but the asshole was still there. I sat there grilling his ass while he looked back at me.

"We're gonna get you."

"Get these nuts, man."

"Funny." He chuckled. "My boss is on her way around here. We'll see who gets the last laugh when she gets on your ass."

I wasn't worried about the murder shit because I knew I was innocent of that. However, he was with the DEA and they were still on my ass. If she was half the bitch he was, she was probably coming with some bullshit. I was only going to entertain her ass for a second because I wanted to put a face with the voice I heard. His boss had to be the female that was at the door of the warehouse that day. There was a knock on the door then the agent got up to open it.

"Let me have the room," the female commanded.

It was definitely the same lady. The agent stepped out then the boss lady sashayed inside. For a second, I sat there stunned because she was so damn pretty. Also, because her ass looked so damn familiar. However, I couldn't place where I knew her from. She smiled as she strutted toward me. I knew I had to be looking at her ass crazy because I was still trying to figure shit out.

"Hello, Em-kay," she spoke, still grinning at me. "It's nice to finally officially meet you."

"For some reason, I feel like this ain't our first meetin'."

"It isn't. My name is Mahogany Dallas. I'm your mother."

Yooo!

One last time...To be continued.

ABOUT THE AUTHOR

Don't want to miss another release?

Subscribe to my mailing list

Connect with the Author

Join Team Turned Out

facebook.com/shameka.jones1

twitter.com/missgemini83

instagram.com/yes.im.that.shameka

AUTHOR LINEAGE

Secret Lovers: what he don't know won't hurt him(4 Book Series)

Turned Out By A Thug (4 Book Series)

Sprung: Turned Out By Love (3 Book Series)

A Hustler's Fantasy (3 Book Series)

No Mercy: Me and My Hitta (2 Book Series)

Infatuated By A Low-Key Boss (3 Book Series)

Turned Out By A Savage (3 Book Series)

Bulletproof Gods: Money Over Everything (2 Book Series)

Saint's Heaven: An Urban Romance (3 Book Series)

Match Made In Heaven: Jug & Tressa's Love Story (2 Book Series)

Turned Out By A Certified Boss (3 Book Series)

A Real One Turned Me Out (3 book series)

In Love With The Plug (1 & 2)

Royalty Publishing House is now accepting manuscripts from aspiring or experienced urban romance authors!

WHAT MAY PLACE YOU ABOVE THE REST:

Heroes who are the ultimate book bae: strong-willed, maybe a little rough around the edges but willing to risk it all for the woman he loves.

Heroines who are the ultimate match: the girl next door type, not perfect - has her faults but is still a decent person. One who is willing to risk it all for the man she loves.

The rest is up to you! Just be creative, think out of the box, keep it sexy and intriguing!

If you'd like to join the Royal family, send us the first 15K words (60 pages) of your completed manuscript to submissions@royaltypub-lishinghouse.com

LIKE OUR PAGE!

Be sure to <u>LIKE</u> our Royalty Publishing House page on Facebook!

CPSIA information can be obtained
at www.ICGtesting.com
Printed in the USA
LVHW090645291019
635575LV00006BA/1042/P